## "I think he's following us..."

"You got a description for me?" he asked.

"Male, six feet tall or slightly less, and very skinny," Skylar said. "His head is covered in a hoodie. Between that and the darkness, I can't see his face."

Tyson looked down at Echo. The dog's body was tensed and ready to spring. Echo's ears twitched toward the figure.

"You sense something?" Tyson whispered to Echo.

The dogs paws tapped the ground, then he woofed softly as if whispering back.

*"Show me."*

### Rocky Mountain K-9 Unit

*These police officers fight for justice
with the help of their brave canine partners.*

**Maggie K. Black** is an award-winning journalist and romantic suspense author with an insatiable love of traveling the world. She has lived in the American South, Europe and the Middle East. She now makes her home in Canada with her history-teacher husband, their two beautiful girls and a small but mighty dog. Maggie enjoys connecting with her readers at maggiekblack.com.

### Books by Maggie K. Black

### Love Inspired Suspense

*Undercover Protection*
*Surviving the Wilderness*

### Rocky Mountain K-9 Unit

*Explosive Revenge*

### Protected Identities

*Christmas Witness Protection*
*Runaway Witness*
*Christmas Witness Conspiracy*

### True North Heroes

*Undercover Holiday Fiancée*
*The Littlest Target*
*Rescuing His Secret Child*
*Cold Case Secrets*

Visit the Author Profile page at LoveInspired.com for more titles.

# EXPLOSIVE
# REVENGE

## MAGGIE K. BLACK

**LOVE INSPIRED** SUSPENSE
INSPIRATIONAL ROMANCE

Special thanks and acknowledgment are given to Maggie K. Black
for her contribution to the Rocky Mountain K-9 Unit miniseries.

LOVE INSPIRED SUSPENSE
INSPIRATIONAL ROMANCE

ISBN-13: 978-1-335-58798-5

Recycling programs
for this product may
not exist in your area.

Explosive Revenge

Love Inspired
22 Adelaide St. West, 41st Floor
Toronto, Ontario M5H 4E3, Canada
www.LoveInspired.com

Printed in U.S.A.

Come unto me, all ye that labor and are heavy laden,
and I will give you rest.
—*Matthew* 11:28

With endless thanks to the fellow authors in this series and all those who've helped us through the year.

# ONE

Sergeant Tyson Wilkes stared at the rows of bright red *X*'s he'd marked on his office wall calendar as if they were a detonation timer counting down the days until the Rocky Mountain K-9 Unit faced its demolition. For almost a year the former army ranger commander had poured every ounce of energy, heart and dedication he had into building a new unit of law enforcement officers, who—along with their fearless four-legged partners—had solved crimes, saved lives and rescued the vulnerable from danger. Now, in just four days' time, his fledgling K-9 family might have everything they worked for snatched away.

And if they did, Tyson knew it would be all his fault.

Today was Monday. On Friday at noon, FBI Special Agent in Charge Michael Bridges, who worked out of the FBI's Denver office, would meet with Tyson to give his assessment of whether the RMKU's year-long trial had been a success or if it would be disbanded due to the relentless stream of sabotage which had put some of their best dogs' lives in danger for the past six months. The sun was setting in a wash of pink and gold, outside his office windows. Most of his colleagues had gone home for the night, and his Dutch shepherd partner, Echo, dozed in his crate with a wheezy snore. Echo's head rested peacefully on his paws just outside the crate's open door. His brown-and-black brindle stripes reminded Tyson of a tiger. It was time to go home and feed Echo. Had to make sure at least one of them got a solid meal and a good night's sleep before getting up tomorrow to start the day over again. As for Tyson, his stomach gnawed but it was like he'd lost his appetite. And he'd had so many sleepless nights, that morning he'd spotted his first bit of gray sneaking into his jet-black hair.

Tyson closed his eyes and pressed his fingers into his temples, where a dull ache built, which ran down his neck and into his back, as if he'd been physically carrying the entire unit and their dogs on his shoulders.

*How can I go home when it feels like everything we've built here is in jeopardy? Dear God, please help me right this sinking ship. If he shuts us down, it'll be all my fault.*

A polite but no-nonsense knock sounded on his office door. Echo's head rose.

"Come in," Tyson called. The door opened, and Officer Skylar Morgan popped her head in. Skylar was still in her crisp black Denver PD uniform with her long auburn hair swept back in a tight bun. Yeah, he remembered what it was like to wear that uniform. He'd been a Denver PD K-9 officer himself before he'd been handpicked to head the RMKU. Skylar was their main go-between with the local police department. For the past several months, she'd been working with them on the case of Kate Montgomery, who for a while had been in a coma following a terrifying car arson where the baby Kate had been taking care of had been kidnapped. Skylar brought an impressive combination of toughness and compassion to the work. Immediately he stood and scanned his ominous calendar for a meeting he might've forgotten. "Skylar, hi. I hope you're here to tell me that Kate has had a breakthrough about the car fire and who might have abducted baby Chloe. I could use some good news."

Kate Montgomery had been found unconscious near her car, which someone had caused to catch fire. An empty infant car seat and baby blanket had been found close to the vehicle—but no baby. The child's mother was found dead in her own car not too far away from the scene. Kate was beginning to get her memory back slowly. She recalled Chloe and her mother but not the circumstances between them. Why had Kate been driving the infant? And to where? Who had wanted to harm them? Who had murdered Chloe's mother? The investigation had been slow going but Tyson felt they were close to solving the mysteries that would lead to baby Chloe's whereabouts.

Skylar's green eyes widened, and he suddenly realized that maybe it was odd for someone to launch straight into a question about a case like that, instead of asking her how she was or trying to make small talk about the lovely fall weather.

But he'd never been one for small talk and couldn't remember the last time he'd thought about anything other than work.

"No, sorry," Skylar said. "But I'm hopeful

that the memory specialist who Kate is working with now is getting her closer to fully remembering what happened."

Tyson nodded. The need to be patient about that case was also wearing on him.

"And I'm sorry to drop in like this," she added. "But I'm struggling with a difficult case and as someone who used to be on the Denver beat yourself, I wondered if you had a moment?"

Tyson glanced at Echo. The dog settled his head back on his paws and closed his eyes again. Looked like he was content to put off his walk and dinner a little longer.

"Absolutely," he said.

"Thank you." Skylar walked into his office and sat down in a chair as he waved her toward it.

Serious green eyes fixed on his face, and despite the fatigue and stress pressing down upon him he felt himself sit up straighter. "What can I do for you?"

Skylar blew out a long breath and he had the odd impression she'd been rehearsing her words on the drive over. Maybe longer.

"A senior on the local high school football team died early this morning of an accidental drug overdose," she said. "This kid was as clean as the day is long, Tyson. He had no idea what he was taking, and he only took half the pill. The buddy who passed it to him thought it was just a run-of-the-mill painkiller he'd gotten from his parents' medicine cabinet and had no idea it was laced with way stronger stuff. Kid didn't even make it to the hospital."

Despite the number of tragedies and deaths Tyson had seen both as a military ranger and cop, he still felt the news of the young man's loss right in the gut.

"How is that even possible?" he asked.

"Counterfeit painkillers are the number one street drug we're dealing with right now," the cop said. Urgency permeated her voice. "We're talking the accidental deaths of construction workers, athletes, injured military vets and people like the dad of the kid who had the pills on him. That man was working a factory job and got a bottle of pills off his supervisor because he couldn't afford to take time off to go to see the doctor, and now a friend of his son is dead."

Tyson sucked in a painful breath. His eyes rose to the picture of his old ranger unit up on his wall and the young men he'd served his country alongside of. Some had come home to do incredible things with their lives. Four of them—Nelson Rivers, Ben Sawyer, Lucas Hudson and Gavin Walker—were now K-9 officers and members of his team. But others had really struggled and getting hooked on meds was part of it.

"It's fraud, Tyson," Skylar said. She leaned forward and he watched as Echo's ears perked at attention as if his K-9 partner understood the importance of what Skylar was talking about. "It's a bait and switch. We've got drug cartels in Mexico creating completely unsafe synthesized pain medication, with a hodge-podge of dangerous chemicals and no controls. You end up with a bottle where one pill has no meds in it at all and the next is so strong it kills you. Then they smuggle it into the state and people literally have no idea what they're taking."

Echo stretched, eased himself out of his cage and quirked his head at Tyson as if the dog somehow knew they needed to act and was awaiting instruction.

"How can we help?" Tyson asked.

He listened as Skylar outlined the overall scope of the Denver PD's current investigation into combating illegal prescription drugs including identifying dealers, arresting criminals and supporting victims. Her briefing was precise, thorough and detailed, while also being incredibly sensitive, and he found himself wishing all of the many briefings he attended were that way.

"Smugglers are using the natural ruggedness of the Rocky Mountains like this huge and impressive hideout to stay off the radar and to stash their money and drugs," Skylar said.

Tyson nodded. "Same thing happens in other parts of the world," he said.

"The Denver police do an amazing job tackling the issue once it breaches our city," Skylar said. "You know that as well as I do. My goal is to stop it from ever getting into our communities by finding the smuggler's next stash while it's still in the mountains. Our sources indicate a new shipment should be arriving any day now. All of our Denver K-9 drug dogs are already working this case from other angles and none have rugged terrain experience. Over the past few months, I've seen the incredible work that your K-9 unit has been doing out in the field. I wondered if you'd consider assigning a K-9 team who understands the Rockies and is experienced in drug detection to help me before it's too late."

Tyson exhaled the breath he didn't realize he was holding. There was exactly one team inside the RMKU who fit that bill and Skylar was talking to them right now. Echo's impressive drug detection skills were singular inside the unit. As for himself, Tyson had experience in working rough, mountainous terrain, as did Echo, since that was exactly where Tyson had found the dog when he'd been overseas in the army. Echo stretched slowly, walked out of his crate and sat beside Skylar. Tyson watched as Skylar's hand instinctively rose to pat his partner, then hovered in the air while she looked over at Tyson as if silently asking his approval. He nodded and Skylar scratched Echo behind the ears.

Tyson glanced at the calendar on the wall with its ominous row of red *X*'s and silently prayed for wisdom. Everything inside him wanted to say yes to her request. Both Echo and he had been stuck in the office too long dealing with the important administration work of running the RMKU for months. His own muscles ached to get back out to doing some hands-on police work and his gut told him that Echo was itching to get out in the field as much as he was. But he had just four days left to prepare for his meeting with

Bridges and to try to get to the bottom of who had been working to sabotage his unit.

If he helped Skylar with this smuggling case, would there even be an RMKU when he was done?

"Also," Skylar continued, breaking the silence first, "I'd like to put in an application to train to become a K-9 officer for this unit once this case is resolved."

He had the impression she'd come prepared to present an impassioned case of why she'd be perfect for his team, but instead her words stopped dead as she met his gaze. Her eyes scanned his face, disappointment flickered momentarily in their beautiful green depths and he realized she must've seen in his expression that he was going to turn her down before he'd even opened his mouth.

"I really wish I could help you with your case," he said, hoping she could read the sincerity in his voice. "But Echo is the only drug detection dog in the unit, and I've got something huge on my plate right now. As for you joining our team, I'm not planning on training any new K-9 officers right now." Not until he knew for certain the unit would be continuing. "But when I do, I'll let you know."

"Thank you for the consideration and your

time," she said and stood. He and Echo stood too. "And if you do ever have time to grab a quick coffee or meal and go over the case further, I'd love to get your perspective."

"Sounds good," he said and nodded non-committally. Skylar had no idea how much he wished he could take her up on it, and not just because he couldn't remember the last time he'd had a decent meal. From the few interactions they'd had over the past few months, she seemed to be a fascinating person and a terrific cop. He'd enjoy picking her mind about the case and bouncing a few ideas around about it. Even if he and Echo couldn't get out there into the Rockies and investigate it with her. But instead he kept that to himself and all he said was "Let me walk you out. I've got to get Echo home for dinner, not to mention some exercise."

Echo's head cocked to the side, with one triangular ear pointing straight up to the ceiling while the other flopped over. Skylar nodded, and Tyson looped the dog's leash around his hand, without clipping it around Echo's harness. He grabbed his coat, and they walked out. The open-floor-plan office was empty, as were the smaller offices that ringed the side of the room. All dogs and their human partners had left for the day, leaving only him and Echo behind. Tyson switched off lights as they went. A cold fall breeze nipped at their faces as they stepped outside.

The parking lot was dark and empty except for his SUV and her police cruiser on the opposite side of the lot. They walked toward her vehicle in silence, with Skylar on his one side and Echo on the other. Each empty space he passed reminded him of just how much his team had changed since their early days almost a year ago, when it seemed like every new member would stay late and try to burn the midnight oil. But over the months, his officers had fallen in love, gotten engaged or married and built families.

Normally, he was more than okay with the fact that his work had overtaken his days and life outside the office had been passing him by. When he'd been serving his country overseas he'd practically slept with his boots on. Maybe it was the fact he'd just turned down a case he was really interested in, the advancing row of red *X*'s on his calendar or something else he couldn't quite put his finger on, but for the first time in a long time Tyson found himself wishing for a life beyond just holding the team together and carrying it on his back.

They reached Skylar's vehicle and he turned to her.

"Thanks for dropping by," he said. "I wish I could do more to help with your case."

A deep engine revved unseen to his right like a monster roaring in the evening gloom. Then blinding headlights split the darkness. A vehicle raced across the lot, picking up speed as it aimed directly for them.

Fractions of a second seemed to stretch into minutes as the vehicle raced toward them. Instinctively Skylar turned and dashed across the parking lot, desperately trying to evade its path. Then she felt Tyson at her side, his hand touching her back as he ran alongside her.

"Jump!" he shouted.

Darkness loomed ahead. She had no idea what she was about to jump into.

One strong arm reached around her waist, half pulling and half guiding her. He leaped and she did too. Their bodies soared over a low barrier fence and tumbled down into a ditch on the other side. His arms wrapped around her, sheltering and protecting her as they rolled. They stopped and for a moment she lay there, stunned from the fall, feeling the protection of Tyson's arms. Then he jumped to his feet and hollered, "Echo! Come!"

She looked up to see the Dutch shepherd leaping majestically through the air as a truck whizzed past, barely missing the tip of the dog's tail. The truck was old, by the looks of it, with a two-seater cab, and was the color of apple juice.

"I didn't see a driver or get a license plate," she said. She climbed shakily to her feet. Only then did she realize that Tyson had reached out his hand to help her up. He pulled it back. "Did you see where he was coming from?"

"No," Tyson said. "It was like there was no vehicle there and then suddenly one appeared."

Yeah, it had been that way for her too. Almost like the driver had been parked somewhere nearby, hiding with his lights off, waiting for them to step outside. But that was a far less likely scenario than it just being some drunk driver who cut through the parking lot by mistake. If she floated her suspicion that the truck had actually been lying in wait, without any proof, would Tyson dismiss her out of hand or think she was leaping to fantastical conclusions?

"Not much to go on when it comes to filing a report," she added. "But I presume you have security cameras?"

If so, that should prove whether the truck had charged down the road or been hiding.

"We do," Tyson said. "But I've got to get to the kennels. Stay close."

"The kennels?" she asked. "Why?"

That was when she realized that Tyson also had his own theories that he wasn't sharing with her.

"Hang on," she said. "What do the K-9 kennels have to do with the near hit-and-run?"

Tyson was already running back up the slope with Echo by his side.

"Long story," Tyson shouted back, "and one I'm not about to get into without evidence."

Right. She followed Tyson out of the ditch and across the dark and empty parking lot.

"I'm calling it in!" she shouted, then grabbed her radio and quickly called in the near miss, giving dispatch the limited information she had. If the driver was drunk or on drugs, they might pose a danger to other pedestrians and motorists, especially if this had just been a random encounter. The dispatcher assured her they'd tell patrol officers to be on the lookout for a pickup truck driving erratically. She ended the call, which had lasted mere seconds, hurried after Tyson and reached him at the door.

"Are they sending an officer out here to take our statement?" he asked.

"No," she said. "I told them the driver was long gone and that we'd both make our own reports about the incident. My main concern was warning patrol officers there was a potential threat on the road."

He nodded. "Good," he said. "Denver PD is stretched thin enough as is. I don't want to waste an officer's time coming all the way out here to ask us what happened when we can look into it ourselves."

The kennels were housed in a large building beside the RMKU's offices, with an outside fenced-in training area around the back. Tyson met a uniformed security guard at the door and exchanged a few words with him out of earshot. But there was no mistaking the deep sigh of relief that seemed to roll off Tyson's shoulders. The guard disappeared back into the building and Tyson waved at Skylar. She and Echo followed him in. They walked through a row of kennels.

"All of our K-9 dogs who've finished training go home with their human partners at night," he said. "We've only got two staying here now. Fortunately, they're both fine."

Again questions filled her mind. A truck

had nearly hit them outside in the parking lot. Why had his instinct been to run inside the unit's training center?

He stopped in front of a kennel where a young black Labrador retriever was curled up in a ball on a blanket.

"That's Shiloh," he said. The relief she'd sensed moments ago filled his voice along with affection for the velvety-eared pup. "Really wonderful dog with a gentle personality. We're all fond of him, especially my assistant, Jodie Chen. But Shiloh is a bit slow in picking up the more ruthless part of training."

"Ruthless?" she asked.

"Maybe that's the wrong word for it," he said and ran his hand over the back of his neck. "There's this certain determination they need, that enables them to ignore all the human emotions swirling around in a situation and simply focus on the task at hand. Some dogs get more distracted by wanting to comfort the victim than charging off after the perpetrator. And Shiloh here is a bit of a softie."

Something in his tone made her wonder if he thought the same was true for human K-9 officers too. Certainly in her experience, too much emotional involvement in someone could cloud a person to what they were really like. Recklessly caring about the wrong person wasn't just foolish; it could be downright dangerous. A yip dragged their attention to the next kennel over. Tyson chuckled softly as they walked over. A small beagle was spinning around in an excited circle.

"And this is Chase," he added. "So much energy but smart as a whip."

Footsteps sounded to their right and they turned to see the security guard had returned.

"I'll just be a minute," Tyson said. "I'm going to see what we've got on the security cameras." He turned to his K-9 partner. "Echo, stay with Skylar. Protect Skylar."

Protect her? From what? She was a cop, and they were alone inside the kennels. Before she could ask anything more, Tyson turned and followed the guard down a hallway. She couldn't help but notice that the kennels, which had been built to house at least two dozen dogs, were practically empty. They clearly weren't overflowing with new recruits. So why had he told her he was putting a hold on new applications? The beagle sniffed around for another moment, then went back inside the crate and started trampling the blankets around in a circle.

Echo looked up at her, tilted his head to

one side and whimpered slightly as if needing something.

"What can I do for you?" Skylar asked the shepherd.

Echo's paws danced, clattering on the hard floor. Skylar didn't know any of the K-9 commands, but she'd been around enough dogs to know when one was in a hurry to go somewhere.

"Outside?" she asked.

The dog woofed, ran a few steps toward the rear of the kennels then back to her. There were too many unknowns swirling around this whole situation to let her guard down fully. She slid her hand onto the handle of her service weapon, ready to unholster it at a second's notice, and slowly pushed the door open to see what looked like a training area, surrounded by a ten-foot chain-link fence. A veritable obstacle course of pylons, hurdles, plastic tunnels and balance beams lay to her left. Another, smaller roped-off area lay to her right. There wasn't another person in sight. The dog trotted outside and started sniffing the ground. Skylar stood there a long moment in the doorway breathing in the night air. It was only then she realized that her heart was racing.

Tyson would never know just how hard it

had been for her to come to him for help. Let alone to risk telling him her dreams of joining the K-9 unit. She had no doubt that he was the best, most qualified person she could've asked for help on the drug case.

Growing up in a house that was full of constant screaming and yelling, she'd thought there were two types of people in the world— the bullies and the weak. As much as she'd loved both her parents, she'd hated the way her father used to drink and rage and how her mother was so hopelessly devoted to his approval and attention she never stood up to him. It was only when it got so bad that neighbors had called the police that she'd realized there was a third type of person too—those who didn't let their emotions take over and instead who protected others. So that's what she'd vowed to be. The three blue words emblazoned on the side of her squad car, Serve and Protect, meant everything to her. When she put on her uniform every day, she was proud to be a protector.

But now, the person she'd come to for help hadn't just turned her down; he'd poured cold water on her hopes of joining his unit. Then after they'd both nearly been run over by someone who for all they knew might've been connected to her drug case, he'd gone to look at the surveillance footage without her and told his dog to protect her. Without explanation. He'd reacted in a way that hadn't made sense to her. She didn't even know why she was as bothered by any of that as she was. Her eyes closed as she prayed that God would help her get past whatever it was that was stirred up inside her. Then she asked for help on stopping the drug smugglers.

Echo barked, prompting her to open her eyes again. It was a short and urgent sound, as if there was something the dog needed immediately. Still standing in the doorway, she glanced back inside the kennels. Tyson was nowhere in sight. She unholstered her weapon and stepped outside, leaving the door open behind her. Floodlights sprang to life behind her, and she wasn't sure if they were motion sensored or if Tyson had seen her on the security cameras and switched them on. A splash of red in her peripheral vision drew her attention to the wall behind her.

She turned and her hand rose to her lips barely stifling a gasp.

A word had been spray-painted on the wall of the RMKU kennels in huge red letters:

RUN.

# TWO

Red spray paint dripped and ran down the kennel's wall like blood. The letters were over six feet high and so fresh they couldn't have been painted more than a few minutes ago. Righteous anger, fear and confusion coursed through her in equal measure. Either the vandal had hopped the tall fence and taken off through the woods or, more likely, had hidden their vehicle in the trees for a quick getaway. She suspected the vandal had been the same person who'd nearly run them over.

Who had done this? And why?

Echo pressed against her leg and whined softly, as if sensing her upset and trying to comfort her. She reached down and ran her hand over the dog's silky ears. Footsteps sounded from inside the building. She turned as Tyson burst through the door and out into the yard. His face was so pale in the flood-lights it almost looked white.

"Are you okay?" Tyson asked. His dark eyes met hers. "What happened?"

She guessed by the angle of the cameras he'd seen her reaction on the camera but not what she'd spotted. She pointed at the wall and watched as his face grew paler. His hand ran over the back of his neck.

"Run?" He echoed the word on the wall under his breath. It was like he was talking to himself. "Now, what does that even mean? Run where? Why? From whom?"

"I don't know," she said.

The slashes of paint were violent and angry. As if someone had attacked the wall with red. She wondered for a moment if it had something to do with either the Kate Montgomery case or even the major drug case which had brought her there. But the message they'd written didn't fit with either.

"Did you call it in yet?" he asked.

"No," she said. "But even though I told dispatch on the last call that we didn't need backup, clearly things have escalated and we need to get a team from the crime lab out here."

"Agreed," he said. "Just hold tight a second. I want to take a quick breath and figure out what's going on first."

This was the second time Tyson had been reluctant to get other investigators involved. Seemed like he was as reluctant to accept help as she was. But was he just independent as she knew a lot of officers could be? After all, he was the leader of the Rocky Mountain K-9 Unit.

Or was there something else going on?

"Did you get anything on the security cameras?" she asked.

"Not a thing," he said. "It's like whoever did this studied the location of our cameras and intentionally targeted the blind spots."

Did that mean this wasn't connected to her drug investigation? If the drug smugglers were onto her investigation and had followed her here as a warning, not only was their message confusing, but how would they know where the cameras' blind spots were?

"My working assumption had been that this is connected to the major drug investigation I'm working on," she admitted. "But if this is a warning to me, I don't know why the criminals chose this word or why the K-9 unit was their target for delivering it."

His eyes were glued to the dripping paint.

"I don't think this has anything to do with your case."

"What?" she asked. She spun toward him, his eyes met hers and she could see the depth of fear and exhaustion brimming there. Oddly her mind flickered back to the calendar on his office wall and the bright red $X$'s that he'd slashed across the days as if he was angry at each one of them. "What do you mean? Is there something else going on that I don't know about? Tyson, are you okay?"

"I'm fine." Tyson broke her gaze. "I'm just dealing with another situation that has nothing to do with your case."

"Is it about Kate?" she asked.

"No."

His response was straightforward and simple but the worry lines on his face told her the case was anything but.

"You want to talk about it?" she asked. "I'm a pretty good listener and bouncing stuff off colleagues always helps me."

She smiled but he didn't.

"I appreciate the thought, but it's the kind of thing I've got to handle on my own," he said.

She nearly chuckled. Yeah, she knew exactly what that impulse was like. But she'd actually overcome it and gotten up the courage to come here and ask his help about her case. She glanced down at his K-9 partner. Echo's quizzical face turned toward her.

"Look, I'm not the K-9 expert," she said, and by the sounds of things becoming one wasn't in her future. "But your partner's the one who dragged me out here after the intruder had left. Echo was very insistent that I needed to see something. So, I just assumed he sensed drug residue."

"Echo's a very special dog," Tyson said. "Sometimes he senses far more than what he learned in his training. We actually met in Afghanistan when he saved my life and a bunch of others in my unit, including four men who are part of the RMKU now."

"Wow," she said. "I'd like to hear that story someday."

Her comment was lighthearted, but as she watched something almost wistful moved behind Tyson's eyes. Instead of replying he looked down at his partner. The dog's feet danced.

"What is it?" Tyson's laser focus turned to his partner, Echo. "Am I missing something? Show me."

Echo barked, in the same sharp and short,

commanding way he had minutes earlier. The dog started running along the wall. Tyson and Skylar followed, jogging to keep up. They reached the very edge of the training area. Tyson pulled his phone from his pocket, switched on the flashlight and shone it up the fence. A piece of olive green fabric was caught in the sharp wire at the top. Echo sat smartly and barked.

"Well, I'll be," Tyson said. "Looks like someone caught their pants on the fence trying to swing their leg over." He looked down at his partner. "Well done. Good job. I think it's time I call this in."

It took less than twenty minutes for the Denver PD to show up. They split up, and she helped search the grounds with crime scene investigators as Tyson went inside the building with detectives. They found what seemed to be drug residue on the torn fabric, and she uncovered an empty spray paint can in the bushes with what looked like a partial fingerprint. While she had no idea how any of this was related to either the warning or the fact the criminal had painted it on the RMKU training center wall, it did mean they had two very good clues toward solving the case and she thanked God for both.

But as the Denver PD team moved out and she prepared to leave, her optimism dimmed when she looked to see Tyson pacing back and forth in front of the building. His phone was pressed to his ear and scraps of his side of what sounded like agitated conversation floated across the lot.

"It's just vandalism... We do, but not that cover that part of the wall... I... I... Yes, Special Agent Bridges... I'll see you Friday. Bye."

Tyson ended the call, glanced up at the dark sky above and seemed to be praying silently. Light and shadows danced down the lines of his face. Then his eyes met hers and she felt herself blush.

"I'm sorry," she said, "I didn't mean to eavesdrop."

"It's okay." He held her gaze for a long and silent moment that seemed to stretch and fill the space between them. "You still up for going to get something to eat?"

Despite a chill in the October air, the line outside the hole-in-the-wall pizza place stretched out the door and down the block. Other guys in Tyson's unit might've bragged about their own state's or city's local pizza, but as far as he was concerned nothing in the world compared to a "Colorado mountain pie." The state's signature deep dish had a dough that was made with honey instead of sugar, and an extra-thick and braided crust to keep the generous toppings from spilling out. And unlike Chicago's similar famous pizza, in Denver a customer could go from seeing their pizza popped into the wood-burning oven to walking out the door with it on a cardboard plate and sheet of wax paper in ten minutes flat.

Light and easy conversation about nothing in particular bounced back and forth between him and Skylar while they waited in line, as they were hardly alone and he wasn't about to start talking about anything work related with strangers crowded around on either side.

Before they'd left, she'd asked if she could use the RMKU female officers' changeroom to get changed into civilian clothes, while he went and fed Echo a mixture of wet and dry food, which was both a lot better for dogs and less exciting than pizza.

When he'd agreed, she'd fished a gym bag out of her car that looked like it was filled with enough clothes and other gear to last most men an entire week. He appreciated people who liked to be prepared.

Now, Skylar was clad in a pair of jeans and a gray sweatshirt. Strands of her red hair fell loose from their bun, and he couldn't help but notice she kept running her hands through them as they talked.

The restaurant owners knew Tyson from way back and had a post out front he tethered Echo's leash to so he could keep his eyes on his partner through the window. As he watched their meat-ladened pizzas cook, he noticed a few empty seats at the window bar and a free but tiny table for two. And while every couple in the place seemed deep in conversation and the handful of solo guys in hoodies and baseball caps scattered around the place seemed even more engrossed in their handheld devices, he also knew none of the stuff he wanted to talk to Skylar about was anything he wanted to risk anyone else overhearing. So he looped Echo's leash around one hand, balanced his pizza pie on the other and they walked down the sidewalk a ways, until they found an empty and well-lit bench in front of a closed clothing store. He was glad to see the store had left its interior lights on to discourage thieves who might try to take advantage of the darkness. He also couldn't help but notice with more than a touch of jealousy that Skylar, who'd had a free hand, unlike him, had been tearing off pieces of crust and nibbling on them as they went.

He knew some K-9 dogs had a hard time tuning out the scents of illegal drugs around them, even when they weren't specifically told to search for them. But Echo was remarkably well behaved and pretended not to notice them, almost as if the dog considered himself undercover. Tyson wondered if Echo was aware of how his right ear would twitch toward certain civilians, giving him away. Tyson sat, let the end of Echo's leash sit loose on the bench and took a bite of pizza so big he was embarrassed as he tried to chew it. Skylar laughed and sat beside him.

"You attacked that thing like you haven't eaten in a week," she said.

He chewed for a long minute, feeling heat rise up the back of his neck, then swallowed.

"I've had a lot on my mind," he said. What's more, he'd been pretty much keeping it all to himself and felt like he hadn't had anyone to confide in. When Skylar had offered him a listening ear, he'd felt something he couldn't begin to put into words leap inside him. Maybe it was true when they said that it was lonely at the top.

It wasn't that he didn't have a terrific team. The officers of the RMKU were a really great group of people and he knew he could've always gone to any of them if he needed someone to talk to. Especially the men he'd served with in the army. But as the boss he'd wanted to help keep morale high, and not worry them with just how hard Bridges was breathing down his neck or heap his own concerns onto them.

Thankfully Echo was an excellent listener. He looked down at his partner. Echo was stretched out in a relaxed but alert position at their feet, with his body resting against Tyson's legs and his head by Skylar's knees.

"You told me Echo was an unusual dog?" she prompted.

"He is." Tyson took another bite, smaller this time, and chewed while trying to decide how to start the story of how the brindle Dutch shepherd had come into his life. He swallowed. "Four years ago, I was leading a team of army rangers in the Middle East," he said. "We were clearing out this empty complex that used to belong to a local warlord. It had been entirely bombed out and all available intel said it was empty. So, we're making our approach to the mansion, just inside the garden walls, when suddenly this beautiful Dutch shepherd comes running through the building toward us barking his head off. But not like a guard dog trying to attack us or send us away. Not at all. More like he was enthusiastically defecting to our side and warning us that we were in danger. Echo was fully grown then, but still had a good bit of puppy in him. We guessed he was about two."

He took another bite of pizza, then leaned down and scratched the dog between the ears.

"Was he right about you being in danger?" Skylar asked.

"Absolutely," Tyson said. "Turned out there was a group of opposing forces hiding in the basement and it was only thanks to Echo here that we didn't walk into a trap. This dog saved our lives."

He heard voices nearby and glanced up. Looked like the pizza place had started to fill up even further, because he could see a handful of customers leaving with their pizza and then loitering around the quiet spot he'd found to eat. Skylar noticed them too. Her keen green eyes scanned the group as if memorizing faces.

Then she leaned her head toward him, like she was about to lay her head on his shoulder, and he felt her hair brush his neck.

"I don't think we're being followed," she said. "But let's take a walk just in case."

He smiled and turned toward her, his heart stuttering a beat to suddenly realize her face was so close to his that they'd almost bumped noses. "I like how your mind works."

He nabbed another bite of pizza, picked up Echo's leash again and stood. So did Skylar. And they continued down the sidewalk.

"Echo followed us around for a while after that," Tyson said. "He'd wander off for days on end and yet he'd always come back to us again."

"Like an echo," Skylar said.

He chuckled.

"Our best guess was that he'd belonged to a private security contractor who'd brought him from overseas and they left him there," he went on. "He was never vicious or violent in any way, so I don't think he was trained as a guard dog. But he had this great intuition, as if he could sense things before I could."

A small playground loomed ahead on the right, in front of a baseball field. It was well lit, thanks to several well-placed lampposts, had good lines of sight, which would discourage anyone from trying to sneak up on them, and was completely empty. Looked like as good a place to stop and finish their pizza as any they were going to find.

"Sounds like he was a natural K-9," she said. She walked over to the swings and sat. He followed. "So, you brought him back when your tour of duty was over and joined the Denver PD?"

"Pretty much," Tyson said. "Although he started training a little bit older than most dogs do."

There was more to the story, but it wasn't the kind of stuff he liked remembering. He dropped Echo's leash again and the dog settled himself down on the grass a few feet away. Tyson sat on the swing beside Skylar, then almost dropped his pizza too as he felt the swing suddenly spin beneath him. Skylar reached over and steadied his pizza. He dug his feet into the dirt and the swing settled.

"Thank you," he said and chuckled. "I don't think these were meant for a man my size."

"We can move to the picnic table?" Skylar suggested.

"Nah, it's okay," Tyson said. Would be nice

to feel like a kid again, instead of a tired man a few years short of forty with hair that was already going gray and the weight of an entire unit on his shoulders. "Actually, to be honest, Echo wasn't my dog back then per se. We all loved him, especially this buddy of mine named Dominic, who was also from around here. We used to joke that when we got back we'd fight over who would train with him."

"Did you ever ask Dominic to join your K-9 team?" she asked.

"Unfortunately, Dominic didn't make it back," Tyson said. He sighed, feeling the sadness of those words wash over him like a tidal wave.

*It was my fault he was in danger and my responsibility to get him out alive. I promised myself I'd never let anyone under my command down again.*

He stared down at the pizza on his lap, feeling his appetite vanish in a second. Suddenly, he felt the swing swaying underneath him. The sound of his own heartbeat filled his ears. Then he felt Skylar's hand brush his arm and the world settled again.

"I'm sorry," she said.

He rolled his shoulders back and she pulled her hand away.

"Anyway," he went on, "after I was discharged, Echo and I entered the Denver PD K-9 program. I couldn't have asked for a better partner. After we assisted FBI Special Agent in Charge Michael Bridges on a major methamphetamine case, he asked me what I thought about creating a Rocky Mountain unit, with handlers who come from K-9 police forces throughout the region, to help the FBI with difficult cases. But the plan has always been to assess the need for the unit after a year. That year's up on Friday."

"And you're worried about it?" Skylar asked.

He turned toward her on the swing, she did likewise and for a moment their knees bumped.

"Very," he admitted. "Six months ago, in April, Officer Ben Sawyer's Doberman partner, Shadow, was accidentally injured in a bite-suit training demonstration I was leading when it turned out the gun was overstuffed with blanks."

Skylar sucked in a breath. "I heard about that."

"I'd handled the gun last," Tyson said, "so it looked like I'd made a major mistake. Either that or someone had somehow breached our armory and overstuffed the blank pistol. Then the keypad entry to the storage room stopped working and I found out there was a slice in the wire insulation leading to the keypad, which must have been how the perps got in. For a while, nothing happened after that and I investigated the sabotage on my own, because everyone else in the unit had some major cases on deck to deal with."

She knew he was talking about the near fatal attack on Kate Montgomery and the kidnapping of the baby girl that had been in her care.

"Then in June," Tyson went on, "almost two months after Shadow was injured and there'd been no other signs of sabotage, the kennel was unlocked and five of the dogs went missing. Two had already been assigned to partners. Another three were new recruits, including Shiloh and Chase, the dogs you met at the training center."

"Hang on," she interjected. "The second attack came two months after the first?"

"Yup," he said. "Odd, right?"

"Very," she concurred.

"Thankfully, we got them all back alive," he went on, "but as I was the one who'd locked up the training center that night, it looked like I messed up. Big-time. Special Agent Bridges called me into a meeting, said he thought the scope of this unit was more than I could handle and told me if I didn't manage to pull things together, he was going to have no choice but to disband the unit. Then in August, our air-conditioning got disabled during a heat wave and several dogs got heat exhaustion."

"Let me guess," Skylar said, "you were the last one in the unit that day?"

"You got it, right on the nose." Tyson tapped his own nose as if to demonstrate. "That time I got an official warning. This Friday, I'll meet with Bridges and he'll pull the trigger on whether or not the unit even continues."

"No wonder you weren't about to take on another case," Skylar murmured.

"And then, tonight, you and I are nearly run down in the parking lot and the wall is vandalized," he said.

"What did the rest of the team think of the sabotage?" she asked. "I presume you assigned some of your team to the case?"

"No, actually," he said. "They're all busy on other active cases so I've been mostly handling this one solo."

He watched as the lines of her forehead crinkled in thought.

Then Skylar's gaze darted past him. Her shoulders stiffened at the same moment he heard Echo begin to growl.

"Don't turn around," Skylar said in a low and warning tone. "But there's a thin man behind us in a black hoodie on the sidewalk. I saw him at the pizza place and again on the street. I think he's following us and by the look of things, he's trying to take our picture."

# THREE

Tension built at the back of Tyson's neck like a steam kettle about to blow as he fought the urge to turn his head and see the person stalking them. But Skylar was right. If he moved too suddenly the man could run. For now, she and Echo had to be his eyes and ears.

"You got a description for me?" he asked, softly.

"Male, six feet tall or slightly less, and very skinny," Skylar said. Her face was inches away from Tyson's as she scanned the man with her peripheral vision. "His head is covered in a hoodie and between that and the fact he's turned his head away from the light and toward the darkness, I can't see his face. But I'm positive he's been following us and that even though he's trying to hide it, he's got his phone's camera trained on us now."

Which meant that even though Tyson's face

was hidden from his camera, the man would have a pretty clear view of Skylar's face. Why was he taking their picture? What, or who, did he want it for? Tyson looked down at Echo. The dog's body was tensed and ready to spring. Echo's ears twitched toward the figure.

"You sense something?" Tyson whispered to Echo.

The dog's paws tapped the ground. Then Echo woofed softly as if whispering back.

"Echo definitely senses something," Tyson told Skylar in a low voice. "One of the quirks of training a dog to detect drugs is sometimes they can't help from letting you know when there's some around even when they're not on duty. With Echo it's like he catches the strain of a melody he can't shake."

Tyson dug his heels into the sand beneath his feet, stood slowly and turned, just in time to see a figure in a black hoodie turn around and hurry away. Now, that was suspicious. Looked like it was now or never. He glanced at Echo and gave the command he knew would get the man off the hook if he had nothing to hide. "Show me."

Echo leaped to his feet with a sharp and re-sounding bark. The man startled, but instead of looking back or hurrying down the sidewalk, he turned on a dime, ran away from the street and across the playing field. In an instant Tyson and Skylar were after him, tossing their pizzas to the ground. Echo ran close by his other side. The dog was disciplined to the core. He wouldn't charge, let alone attack, without a direct command. Tyson reached for his badge, which he kept on a lanyard around his neck and tucked inside his jacket. But Skylar got to hers first.

"Officer Skylar Morgan, Denver PD!" Skylar shouted. She held her badge in front of her as she ran. "You're not in any trouble. We just want to talk."

But the figure wasn't about to slow. He was limping slightly, Tyson noticed, as if his left ankle was stiff. But it didn't seem to slow him down, which implied the injury wasn't new. Tyson watched as he reached a chain-link fence, leaped up it and then threw himself over the top, practically falling to the ground on the other side. Something Tyson couldn't quite see tumbled from the man's pocket. Whatever it was, either the attacker didn't notice or decided it wasn't worth stopping to retrieve. Echo's barks rose as the man disappeared into the darkness. Tyson reached the fence and was about to climb when he heard a truck engine roar and saw headlights flash.

The suspect was getting away. Frustration poured over him and he channeled into prayer for God's help.

Skylar dropped to one knee in the grass, turned her phone's flashlight on and shone it on the ground on the other side of the fence.

"He dropped something," she said. He watched as she pulled the end of her sweat-shirt over the tips of her fingers like a glove and squeezed her hand through the chain link. She felt around in the grass. "Do you have an evidence bag? Gloves? Anything like that?"

"I've got a roll of baggies," he said. Wouldn't be much of a responsible dog owner if he didn't always have both plastic bags and treats on him. He fished them out of his pocket, tore one off and handed it to her.

"Thanks." She slid her hand into the bag like a glove, reached through the bars again and before he could even suggest climbing the fence instead, she pulled her hand back out again and held what she'd found aloft. It was a small plastic baggie. At first glance it seemed empty. Then he saw some grains of white residue and what seemed to be part of a pill.

"Voilà!" she said and stood. "We've got something that sure looks like drugs."

Echo barked triumphantly.

"Sure sounds like Echo agrees with you," Tyson said.

"Pass me another bag?" she asked. He did so and she used it like a second glove and opened the baggie carefully. She smelled it and then held it out to Tyson. "I'm not about to taste it," she said. "But I'm pretty certain this is the same stuff as the fake prescription pills I'm trying to track. Which makes him either a dealer or user."

"Or both," Tyson said.

"Are we agreed in believing that whoever this man is he's not the big criminal mastermind who's been running a large-scale drug organization but could be one of his lower-level henchmen?" she asked.

"I feel pretty comfortable coming to that conclusion," he said. "Whoever is out there running a drug operation large enough to be flooding Denver with counterfeit pills smuggled in from Mexico is very unlikely to be doing his own grunt work. This guy was clearly taking pictures of us, and I feel safe to assume it was for someone else."

He ran his hand over the back of his head.

"When that truck had come out of nowhere and nearly run us over back at headquarters, my immediate reaction was to dash to the kennels and make sure the dogs were all right. I presumed from the very beginning that both the attempted hit-and-run and the ominous warning painted on the side of the kennels were done by whoever had been causing me trouble and targeting my unit for the past few months. Special Agent Bridges definitely thought so too. When he heard there was an incident at the RMKU tonight he called and read me the riot act. But what if I was wrong? What if this is about your drug case?"

She slid the clear baggie into one of Tyson's bags and tied it shut.

"What if they're linked?" she said. "You and Echo worked a lot of drug cases back when you were with the Denver PD. Maybe somebody you put away in the past is coming after you."

"Maybe," he said. He had a whole lot of maybes. What he needed was answers. But he didn't exactly have a lot of extra time to gather them on top of preparing for Friday's meeting. "I hate to ask this, considering I remember the hours cops work on your beat, but are you free to meet up and compare our thoughts on this case, after your shift tomorrow night? Say around five thirty? We might have more information on everything that happened tonight."

Her green eyes met his and widened. They were beautiful, he realized, with flecks of gold and long, thick lashes.

"We could go over your case as well," he added quickly, "and the sabotage at the kennels. Two heads are better than one, and if we compare notes we might find some answers. If we solve your case, and it turns out that is what everything that happened at the kennels tonight was about, it'll helpfully get Bridges off my back. And if, on the other hand, you help me crack who's behind the ongoing sabotage at the kennels before my meeting with him later this week, you might just help me save the unit."

She held his gaze for a long moment. Something he couldn't quite read flickered in her eyes. Then she smiled. "Deal," she said. "You bring any case files you've got on anyone who might have a grudge against the RMKU. I'll bring my recent drug files and dinner."

Butterflies danced in Skylar's stomach Tuesday night as she walked across the parking lot to the sizeable RMKU headquarters, with her bag of files slung over one shoulder and two glass casserole containers balanced in her hands. One was filled with fresh meatballs and the other with homemade buns. She'd always loved cooking. There was something both fun and relaxing about kneading the dough, shaping the buns with her palms and watching them rise and become golden in her bread maker, before then mixing the meat and spices by hand and stacking the small round balls in her slow cooker. Then she'd head off to work, knowing when she got home she'd have the hot, cozy and delicious aromas waiting for her.

But there'd been something different about this meal. She'd second-guessed herself about each ingredient she added and then spent all day at work worrying about what it would taste like. Then when she'd gotten home to find with relief that the food was great, she'd started overthinking which top she should wear with her jeans and whether she should touch up her makeup.

It was ridiculous. She'd met up with various friends and colleagues after work more times than she could count. Sergeant Tyson Wilkes was a strong, smart and dedicated colleague.

She respected him deeply and was thankful for the opportunity to work with him. It was something she'd prayed for, because she'd hoped that he'd have the insight she needed to stop the drug smugglers. So, she didn't know where the weird fluttering in her heart and odd nerves were coming from. All she knew was she didn't like them.

*Lord, help me be strong and to discard anything inside me that's making me weak. For the sake of both Tyson's unit and my case.*

This time she found Tyson and Echo standing outside the front door, with the tall and muscular form of K-9 Officer Ben Sawyer and his equally imposing Doberman partner, Shadow, who specialized in protection. Skylar had met Ben back in the spring, when he'd been assigned to protect a beautiful wildlife photographer named Jamie, who'd been a key witness in a Denver PD murder trial. Ben and Jamie had not only stopped a killer, but they'd also fallen in love, gotten married and were now raising Jamie's baby daughter, Barbara June.

Despite everything she'd faced the night before, she immediately felt safer seeing them there.

Ben tipped his cowboy hat in greeting as she approached.

"Good evening," he said. "We've all been talking about what happened here last night, and all the other sabotage we've been dealing with. Tyson was just telling me you're working on a drug case you think might be connected?"

It was good, but not surprising, to know that Tyson's team had his back.

"Sure am," she said. "Hopefully, if we put our heads together on this we'll figure out what's going on."

The three of them said their goodbyes, Ben promised to give Jamie her best, then he sauntered off to his vehicle with Shadow by his side.

Tyson turned to Skylar.

"Thanks for coming," he said. "I really appreciate it."

"No problem," she said.

She held up the containers and his eyes widened at the sight of the food in her hands.

"That looks amazing," he said.

"Just meatballs and buns," she said, "with a bit of melted cheese. Figured we could make sandwiches."

"Again, amazing," he said. "I'd have been happy with a peanut butter sandwich."

Then his eyes met hers and she felt a flush of heat brush her cheeks.

"Don't knock peanut butter sandwiches," she said. "Did you pull the files?"

"Yup," he said. "There's only a few, because the RMKU is only a year old. But as you'll see I've already gathered a lot of information about the ongoing situation. And while I don't have access to my specific Denver PD files from before I joined the unit, I did take extensive notes on all my past cases, which I still have."

"Better to have too much information than not enough," she said.

"Agreed," he said. "But we might be in for a long one."

After they'd worked a full shift, she thought.

Then as if reading her mind he added, "I've made coffee."

She followed him through the RMKU headquarters. Most of the glass-walled offices were empty. But Tyson stopped by one and waited as the officer inside wrapped up a phone call.

A moment later, the officer rose from his desk to greet them. He had short black hair and a scar above his left eyebrow that seemed to accentuate the intensity of his striking blue eyes.

"Chris Fuller," he said, then glanced down as a white-and-brown spaniel popped his head inquisitively around the corner. "And this is my partner, Teddy. He specializes in tracking."

Chris reached out his hand toward Skylar.

"You're Officer Morgan, right?" he added. "I've seen you around, but I don't think we've ever been properly introduced."

"Call me Skylar." She took his hand and shook it, before stepping back.

"All good?" Tyson asked Chris.

"Yeah, I was just on the phone with Lucas," Chris said. "He was filling me in on how things are going."

"Lucas Hudson and his partner, Angel, specialize in search and rescue," Tyson explained, turning to Skylar. "They're currently in Montana. Chris and Teddy were in Montana a few months back tracking an escaped convict, so he's been giving Lucas the lay of the land."

He turned back to Chris.

"Sounds good," Tyson said. "Keep me posted and don't stay too late. It's important to get enough rest."

"It's okay," Chris said. "I've got a bunch to catch up on and warned Lexie that tonight might be a long one."

Tyson and Skylar moved on, and they were almost at the kitchen when Tyson added, "Chris is a newlywed. Lexie's a pilot. They met in Montana."

He said it almost apologetically as if wanting to explain why he wasn't keeping his own advice.

They reached the small staff kitchen, where they assembled sandwiches, transferred them onto mismatched plates and grabbed a roll of paper towels to serve as napkins. When they reached Tyson's office, she blinked to see dozens of yellow lined notepads scattered across his desk.

"Wow, here I was feeling a bit bad for bringing over this many files, but you really weren't joking when you said you made a lot of notes," she said.

"I prefer paper," he said. "Something I can touch, feel and jot down notes on."

"What are we looking at?" she asked.

"These six contain notes about all the drug cases I worked on where anyone might hold a grudge," he said. "These four are everything I've got on what's been happening around here and this notepad contains what I know so far about the current fake prescription drug case. I've been doing my homework since yesterday." He clocked her gaze as she scanned the notepads. "Overwhelming?"

"Nah," she said. "Thrilling, actually. Thank you for sharing all this with me. I can't wait to get into it."

"Well, I'm equally excited to read through everything you've brought," he said. "I'm sure you know a lot that I don't."

She felt a smile cross her face that was matched only by the size of the grin on his own.

Then he chuckled. "And here I was afraid of scaring you off."

"Never," she said. She set her plate of food down on a tiny corner of free space on his desk, then reached into her own bag, pulled out the stack of files she'd brought and handed them to him over the pile. "Here's where I'm at in the current drug smuggling case. I've got maps, interviews, satellite footage, the whole shebang."

"I can't wait," he said.

They sat down on opposites sides of the desk and began to read. There'd been no progress in tracking down the apple juice–colored truck which had almost run them down Monday night or the man with the limp they'd seen taking their picture. But they were also pretty sure whoever that man was he'd been working for the drug kingpin of the smuggling operation Skylar was investigating.

They agreed when it came to identifying the kingpin, they were looking for anyone who'd been in jail for drug offenses, had been recently released and who had reason to have a grudge against Tyson. Bonus points if they stumbled upon someone who'd also received visits in prison in April, June or August by someone who might be the henchman with the limp.

A comfortable silence fell between them, which stretched from minutes into an hour, as they picked up files, scanned the information, made notes on their respective notepads and then reached for the next, in between bites of meatball subs and fresh cups of coffee. For a while, Echo lay on the floor between them, ready to spring into action if called upon or to chase any loose meatballs that went flying. But eventually he gave up, walked into his kennel and curled into a ball. The dog's wheezing snore filled the space.

"When you were investigating the ongoing sabotage at the kennels," Skylar asked, "what did you make of the schedule of the attacks?"

Dark eyebrows quirked over even darker eyes.

"What do you mean?" he asked.

"We've got incidents happening in April, June, August and now in October," she said. "Whoever's doing this is spacing the attacks out two months apart."

Tyson blinked. "I hadn't pegged that," he said. "Each attack was so different and disconnected I didn't realize there might be something intentional in the spacing."

"Also, I can see why you didn't assume they were connected to an old drug case," she said. "The first incident was six months after Bridges gave you authorization to start the Rocky Mountain K-9 Unit. Halfway into your one-year trial is an odd time to start trying to sabotage you. Can you remember what case you were working on then?"

"It was around the time Kate Montgomery was found unconscious at the car fire," he said, "and we realized a baby had been kidnapped. The team is working so hard on that case, but there is no sign of little Chloe Baker."

Skylar closed her eyes for a moment, praying silently for the woman fighting to regain her memory of what happened the night baby Chloe had been taken.

"It's possible the vandalism is connected to that case," he said, "but…"

"But it doesn't feel right?" Skylar asked.

"Yeah," he admitted. "Cases have a pattern and logic to them. There's a reason why criminals do what they do. This doesn't seem to fit. Whoever stole that baby took great pains to hide their actions. This sabotage is by someone trying to make a statement."

"I agree," she said. "But there was a lot of media attention on the missing baby case at the time. Maybe someone with a grudge saw the coverage and decided it was time to come after you."

"Agreed," he said and nodded.

"Whoever's after you did their homework," she added. "Who knows how long they'd been watching you."

"True," Tyson said. "Also I can't shake the memory of that guy pointing a camera at us last night. Maybe he's working for someone besides the drug kingpin who paid or coerced him into surveilling us."

The idea unsettled him, especially if Skylar's proximity to him put her life in danger. They lapsed back into silence. Another hour passed and then a second, until she looked up at the clock and realized it was almost ten. So did Tyson.

"Whoa," he said. "I'm sorry. I've completely lost track of time and Echo and I have got to be up at five tomorrow."

She stood slowly and stretched the aches out of her body. "Yeah, I've got an early morning too. We should probably compare notes and then call it a night."

"Agreed."

Tyson went first, spreading the files she'd provided him out on the table and identifying some areas in the mountains that he felt the smugglers were most likely to be using as a hideout. Then they talked through their thoughts on his previous drug cases, narrowing it down to criminals who'd threatened his life, were in the area and had exhausted their legal avenues of appeal.

"I've narrowed it down to a handful," Tyson said. "One of them got so mad he tried to both punch and stab me while I was arresting him. Another torched his entire drug operation while we were closing in, in an attempt to destroy the evidence. But no one on the list leaps out as a main suspect yet."

"Give me the list and I'll look into them further," Skylar said. "Maybe I'll come up with something. Also, several of your other K-9 officers used to work for other police forces. Maybe this person's not targeting you specifically but the unit more generally. I'll put together some files that match our other criteria, but where you weren't personally involved in the arrest. I could drop them by tomorrow, but I'm afraid I have a meeting after work, so won't be free until after eight."

"I'll be here," he said.

They left the files in neat stacks on the top of his filing cabinets, cleaned their dishes in the kitchen and then headed out into the parking lot. Skylar felt her footsteps drag as they crossed the empty lot and for reasons that weren't just fatigue. She couldn't remember the last time she'd enjoyed just spending hours going over files. While they hadn't walked away with any concrete solutions, she just hoped all the work they'd done had helped get them one step closer to finding the answers.

Tyson pulled his keys from his pocket and rolled them around between his fingers. "This was great," he said. "Now we've both got some solid leads to chase."

"And I'm still waiting on the Denver PD crime lab to return their analysis of the evidence we collected yesterday," she added. "There might be more leads there."

"Hopefully," he said. His K-9 SUV and her

police car were parked at opposite sides of the lot. He spun the keys around in his fingers again as if he wanted to ask her something more but couldn't find the words. He leaned down and ran his hand over the back of Echo's head.

"I'm looking forward to seeing the files you bring over tomorrow," he said. "Hopefully there'll be something actionable there. Also, when I meet with Special Agent in Charge Michael Bridges on Friday, if all goes well there, I'll see what I can do about allocating some resources your way."

"Sounds good," she said. "Have a good night."

She turned and started walking across the parking lot toward her vehicle. He walked to his and pressed the button on his key fob. Something clicked. Then his SUV exploded in a ball of fire.

# FOUR

The blast ripped through the air with such force it knocked Tyson off his feet. He felt himself being tossed backward through the air. Then his body smacked hard against the pavement. Pain shot through him. He pushed himself up on his grazed palms and scanned the scene. Bright orange flames engulfed his K-9 SUV. Pitch-black smoke billowed, and the harsh smell of gasoline filled the air.

He couldn't see his K-9 partner or Skylar anywhere.

"Echo! Come!" He summoned his partner and then called out, "Skylar! Where are you?"

He prayed, *Please, Lord, let them be okay.*

Echo burst through the haze of smoke and leaped to his side. The dog's nose nuzzled his cheek protectively and Tyson winced as he felt the sharp pain of something like shrapnel in his jaw.

"Tyson!" Skylar's voice called from somewhere to his right. "Over here!"

He climbed to his feet and saw her. She was crouched on the pavement beside her car and holding her radio to her ear. He prayed and thanked God.

"You all right?" he called.

"Yeah!" she said. "I'm on the phone with dispatch. Fire trucks are on their way. You okay?"

"I'm fine," he said.

He slowly made his way across the parking lot to her, keeping his body low. Skylar's bright green eyes met his through the swirling soot.

"They'll be here in three," she said. "Meanwhile we've gotta move back."

"I've got a fire extinguisher in my office—" he started.

But she cut him off. "Forget it. It's too late for that."

His neck stiffened. As a former army ranger commander and now the head of the RMKU, he had people disagree with him all the time. But he couldn't actually remember the last time someone had the temerity to just cut him off like that. "We need to put out the fire—"

"The blaze is already out of control," Skylar said. Urgency permeated the cop's voice. "So, unless you've got a spare fire truck stashed under your desk there's nothing we can do."

He opened his mouth, not certain whether to argue or laugh. For the first time in longer than he could remember he couldn't think of any words to say. What's more, he knew she was right.

Distant sirens filled the air as the three of them made their way away from the fire and around to the far side of her car. Shouting sounded from behind them, and he looked through the haze to see the building security guard running toward them, along with Chris and his partner, Teddy.

Tyson hadn't realized Chris had stayed at work so late.

Chris's phone was to his ear, and Tyson could hear he was calling things in to 911 as well. But as he neared, Chris pulled the phone from his ear.

"Everyone all right?" Chris called. Urgency filled his voice.

"We're all good," Tyson reported. "No injuries."

"Dispatch tells me that emergency services

are already on their way," Chris said. "How can I help?"

"Is there anyone left in the building?" Tyson asked.

"No," Chris said, "I'm pretty sure we're the last ones here."

"Double-check and ask anyone you find who's still in the building to stay inside," Tyson told the security guard, "and get me any security footage you can that might show us what happened."

Then he turned to Chris. "Check the perimeter in case whoever did this is lurking around."

"Got it!" Chris turned and ran back toward the building, as did the security guard.

Moments later, Tyson saw the flashing red-and-white lights as fire trucks flooded the parking lot, along with K-9 Officer Nelson Rivers's SUV.

Nelson jumped from his vehicle and ran toward them, along with his yellow Lab partner, Diesel, who specialized in detecting flammable accelerants. They reached Tyson and Skylar before the fire trucks had even fully parked.

"What happened?" Nelson asked. "I heard

a call come through the police scanner about a fire at this address and rushed straight over."

Tyson silently thanked God for his team.

"My vehicle exploded," he said. "That's all we know right now. Chris and Teddy are doing a perimeter sweep, if you want to join them and see if Diesel can sniff out anything. The last thing we want is to miss a secondary explosion, and I don't know there's much else we can do until the fire is out."

"Got it," Nelson said. He and his partner started toward the back of the RMKU.

Tyson and Skylar ran over to the closest fire truck, where he and Skylar quickly briefed the captain in tandem—after all, it was his vehicle and she was the one who'd made the call—as firefighters unfurled their hoses and prepared to battle the flames. Tyson couldn't remember the last time he'd briefed an emergency crew alongside another officer. And even though it only took seconds, he couldn't help but be taken aback at how easily the verbal patter and teamwork seemed to flow between them. Especially considering he and Skylar had just disagreed moments before. It felt like they had been working together for years. He also noticed the precision and clarity in her words and the way she got immediately to all the significant points.

Yeah, Skylar was definitely the kind of person he'd happily serve alongside on a case. Or even go into battle with.

He, Skylar and Echo retreated back to the front of the building and watched as the firefighters drenched his car and the surrounding ground in the thick fire suppression foam used specifically on accelerant fires when pressurized water risked spreading the flames. The flames seemed to burn even brighter now with red-and-orange peaks rising from within the thick black smoke. White clouds of foam broke off from the stream and floated through the air toward where Tyson stood, with Skylar to one side and his hand on Echo's collar.

Then it was all over and the firefighters were rolling up their hoses again. Tyson sighed as he glanced at the foam-covered charred remains of his K-9 SUV, then oddly remembered just how long it had taken him to get a new unit vehicle for Gavin Walker, his last recruit—an entire week.

Echo whined softly as if realizing just how many chewy toys and soft blankets he'd just lost in the blaze. Tyson ran his hand over his neck and scratched him behind his ears.

"Don't worry, buddy," he whispered. "I got your back, and I'll make sure you're covered."

The fire chief came over and they exchanged a few more words. As far as the firefighters could tell the fire had been caused by the combination of a homemade explosive and some kind of gasoline accelerant attached to Tyson's gas tank. But crime scene and forensic investigators would be able to tell them more when they processed the vehicle and would be bringing a trailer to take Tyson's vehicle to the crime lab's garage.

Chris and Nelson returned with their partners to report that neither had found any trace of an intruder on-site or any additional accelerants. By this time, Tyson's phone had been ringing off the hook with calls from other members of the K-9 unit offering to help and asking what they could do. This included a call from Gavin, who was a couple of hours away on another case with his explosives detection dog, Koda, but offered to drive back immediately if Tyson needed him.

Tyson thanked them all but told them he was now at the stage of passing the scene on to the care of Denver PD's forensic investigators. While he deeply appreciated their concern, the most frustrating thing for Tyson was that in this specific instance there wasn't much any of them *could* do right now—including himself. And the knowledge of that ate away at him. There were no suspects to interview, the perimeter had already been thoroughly searched by the dogs, and as for examining the remnants of his vehicle, that was a job they'd have to leave up to the crime scene investigators.

The threat against him had escalated from sabotage of the K-9 kennels and equipment to actual violence. And yet, in this moment there was nothing for Tyson to do but wait for the crime scene investigators and forensic team to do their job.

So, he thanked his team, told them there was no need for them to come down, and sent both Nelson and Chris home to their wives.

Then Tyson glanced to the dark sky above and silently prayed.

*I don't know what's happening or why the unit and I are under attack. Please help me figure out what's going on, before it's too late.*

Skylar walked over to him.

"Okay, I got off the phone with the crime

lab," Skylar said. "They should be here in the next twenty minutes or so to take the vehicle away and see if there's any other evidence they can glean. They apologize for the delay."

"It's okay," he said. The lab would be closed for the night, which meant they'd be bringing in the on-call team. "It's late and I'm guessing you start as early in the morning as I do. I've already told the rest of my team there's not much left to do here tonight but wait. So, if you want to head out and go home, I don't mind holding down the fort."

"Nah, I'm good," she said. "I'm the officer who called it in. Plus, someone's gotta stick around to give you a ride home considering your car's extra crispy."

Despite the stress, worry and fear that had been weighing him down, he found himself chuckling. There was just something about her. Like a positivity in the face of a crisis, wrapped in a wry sense of humor.

His late grandfather would've called it pluck.

"Deep-fried with a poor excuse for whipped cream," he said.

She laughed. He ran his hand over his face, then winced as sharp pain filled his jaw. In all the chaos he'd forgotten about the shrapnel feeling he'd gotten when Echo had nuzzled his face.

"Your cheek is bleeding," Skylar said. She caught hold of his fingers as he pulled his hand from his face. Concern filled her voice that was somehow both in stark contrast to the authoritative and professional police tone she'd used just moments earlier, and yet somehow equally her.

"It looks like some tiny shards of glass from the windshield got caught in your skin," she said. "I didn't notice until you just rubbed your face. Thankfully I have a first aid kit in my car." She walked to her car, opened the driver's-side door, reached across the seat and grabbed a first aid kit from the glove compartment.

"I'm fine," he said, almost automatically and as if she hadn't just seen him wince. "They're just slivers. They'll probably fall out on their own."

Back when he was in the military, it was almost as if he and his fellow army rangers prided themselves in not going to see the medic if they could possibly muscle through.

She nodded as if she'd heard him, then said, "Yup, or they'll get worse." Then she straightened up and gestured to the driver's seat. "Now, have a seat and it'll only take me a second."

Almost to his own surprise, he sat with his feet out on the pavement. Echo sat neatly beside him, as if curious to watch the proceedings.

"You know, back in the rangers when you get cut you just slap some duct tape or glue over it and get right back out into battle," he said.

"That's how you get infections," she said.

Her gentle fingers ran over his jaw, feeling for the glass.

"And scars," he said. "I hear some women find them handsome."

Her eyes widened in mock surprise. There was both a strength and a softness to their green depths, he realized, like the beautiful and vibrant green mosses of the Rocky Mountains which protected the rock from erosion.

"Oh, I didn't realize you were trying for scars. In that case, just give me a second and I'll go find some more shards for you."

He laughed. She pulled a pair of tweezers from her first aid kit, then set the kit down on the roof of the car. Who was this woman? One moment she was the perfect law enforcement officer. The next it was like they'd been best friends for years. And somewhere in between she was disagreeing with him. Her left hand brushed the side of his face and gently tilted it up toward the car's interior light. Then he felt the scrape of the tweezers against his cheek, the quick tug of something being pulled from his skin and the odd sense of relief as the foreign object left his face. Then her tweezers touched his face a second, third and fourth time, slowly and methodically pulling the near-invisible irritants from his skin. And he realized if she hadn't insisted on helping he'd have probably gone for days, or even weeks, not knowing why his jaw hurt while being too busy to see a doctor. Finally, he felt the smooth and gentle touch of her fingertips brush over his cheek and down over the lines of his jaw, sending shivers through his skin.

"I think we're good," she said, softly.

Then her eyes met his, and he realized with a jolt it was the first time, in a long time, his face had been just inches away from a woman's. All either of them would've had to do was tilt their chin just a few inches and their lips would have met in a kiss.

More headlights burst through the night

behind them. Skylar stepped back and sighed in relief.

"The CSIs are here," she said. "Finally. Now all we have to do is wait for them to wrap it up and we can get out of here. At this rate, I might even still manage to read a bit before bed and still get seven hours' sleep."

She turned and walked toward the approaching vehicle, leaving him to wonder if the awkward tenderness that had just passed between them a moment before had just been in his own head.

He stood up, closed the car door and looked down at Echo. His partner's large eyes looked up at him.

"Don't worry," he said, mostly to the dog but also if he was honest a little bit to himself. "I've got my eye on the ball and I'm completely focused on the case, the unit, preparing for my meeting with Special Agent Bridges about the future of RMKU and convincing him to make us permanent. Nothing is going to distract me from that."

Not even whatever the weird feeling was that fluttered like moths trapped in his chest.

He and Echo strode across the parking lot. Tyson shook hands with the lead CSI investigator, noting with some irony it was the same team who'd been out there the night before.

"Don't worry," he said, "I promise we won't make this a daily occurrence."

The lead investigator smiled politely.

The forensic team went to work. The scene was processed, his vehicle was taken away and within less than half an hour, he, Skylar and Echo were left alone in the parking lot again.

"Well, guess that's it," Skylar said.

She barely managed to stifle a yawn and then flushed as she met his eyes and realized he'd noticed. He glanced at his watch—almost two hours had passed since they'd first walked out to the parking lot.

"Weird thing is I don't feel tired yet," he admitted. "I still have enough adrenaline coursing through my system that I feel like I could keep going for hours. I suspect that when fatigue does catch up with me it'll slam into me like two thousand pounds of bricks."

She stopped and turned to him. "Why two thousand pounds?"

"Because that's a ton," he said, with a grin. "Once when I was a kid I took a brick from the driveway and tried to weigh it on my mother's kitchen scale to figure out exactly how many bricks were in a ton. Unfortunately her little spices scale wasn't intended for bricks and I broke it."

She laughed. "You're fantastic."

She opened the back door for Echo, Tyson got in the passenger's seat and then she got in the driver's seat.

"Please go ahead and program your address into the computer GPS," she said, and he did so. "I'm sorry I don't have a doggie seat belt for Echo."

"It's okay," Tyson said, "I have one at home I can bring for next time."

*Next time*, he thought. Why had he just said that?

They drove in silence through the dark and beautiful roads of Denver to the small bungalow he and Echo shared. It was a comfortable silence. Like old friends or fellow soldiers in a battle.

"I'd love to hear more about your time as an army ranger," she said, after a long moment.

"Not much to tell," he said. "It was a lot of grunt work and nothing too impressive. Mostly we just kept the peace."

When she pulled the car to a stop, he glanced out to see his own front door and was surprised to realize the drive home had somehow seemed so much shorter than usual. Skylar chuckled under her breath and he had no idea what he'd said that was funny.

"So many people try to exaggerate their accomplishments," she said. "You, on the other hand, like to downplay how impressive you are. Let me guess, you're also the kind of person who carries all the weight of keeping the unit alive, but none of the credit when you succeed."

He opened his mouth. But no words came out. He didn't know if she meant his army rangers unit or the RMKU. Either way, she wasn't wrong. He undid his seat belt.

"Well, thank you for the ride," he said, "and for having my back tonight. I really appreciate it."

A beautiful smile lit up her face. "Anytime."

Then before he'd stopped to think about what he was doing, he leaned across the front seat, wrapped his arms around her and hugged her goodbye.

Their fleeting hug goodbye probably hadn't lasted more than a second, maybe two. Yet, Skylar had replayed it in her head for hours that night when she should've been sleeping. Only to then wake up the next morning and find the memory of Tyson's strong arms around her had continued to run through her mind all day, as she patrolled the streets, interviewed suspects, reviewed files and chased up potential leads on her drug case. How had they ended up hugging like that? Had he reached for her? Had she reached for him? Or had they both somehow instinctively leaned forward and wrapped their arms around each other like two close friends who'd both gone through a long and exhausting evening together?

She had no idea and maybe that's what bothered her most of all, along with just how normal and simple it had felt to have his arms around her. Comfortable and safe, and like she'd imagined home would feel if her own childhood home had ever been either of those things. She had very few memories of hugging her parents, and those hugs she did remember were awkward and distant. She'd never seen her parents hug, kiss or show any kind of affection to each other.

Her shift ended at five and she left with a fresh box of files to give to Tyson, as promised, which matched the criteria they'd agreed upon. Most days, she stuck around the precinct for a while, putting in overtime and trying to tie up loose ends. But instead she ran home to change out of her uniform, transferred the box of files into the trunk of her civilian car and then drove to a large community church in the middle of downtown. It had been a couple of years since she'd started attending her church's weekly Wednesday-night support for friends and families of addicts.

At first, she'd worried that the other members of the group would think she didn't belong.

Yes, she'd rarely seen her father without a drink in his hand and even now her mother relied on pills. And yes, they'd fought nonstop when she was a kid and that had been scary. But as a cop, she'd also known that many other people had far worse stories, and had seen their parent, spouse, children or friend wreck their lives and end up on the streets, in hospital or in jail. So she'd told herself that other people needed the help of support groups more than she did and that she was fine on her own.

But then she'd agreed to go with a friend from church whose daughter had been arrested for drunk driving. To her surprise, Skylar had found herself surrounded by welcome, encouragement and support. And while some of them had life experiences that were very different than hers, she'd learned a lot from their stories and their wisdom and always left feeling refreshed. Not to mention, as someone who often battled the temptation to be a workaholic, it was nice to have the weekly reminder to maintain balance in her life.

She parked her car across the street from the church, in front of a small strip mall. Groups of two and three clustered in the church parking lot. As she crossed the street, she couldn't help but notice a couple of people lurking around the area who her cop instincts told her were up to no good. Her lip curled in disgust. It infuriated her how drug dealers would hang around the very places where people went to get help, like piranhas circling a school of vulnerable fish, trying to exploit people's pain and need. She reminded herself that she was off duty, right now it wasn't her job and that her brothers and sisters in blue would be patrolling the area. As if on cue, she watched as a white-and-blue Denver PD police car rolled slowly down the street and the miscreants in front of the mall scattered.

*Thank You, Lord. When I walk into that*

*room, help my heart be open to listening to
the stories of others and receive whatever
You have for me.*

She shut off her phone, walked into the
church and found a seat. About three dozen
people sat in surprisingly comfortable metal
chairs. There were men and women of all
walks of life, ranging in age between teen-
agers and eighties, brought together by love
and worry for those they cared about.

"I tried to convince myself that pills were
safer than alcohol or other kinds of drugs,"
a man who looked about fifty, with a salt-
and-pepper beard and worn jeans, said to the
group. "Because I told myself as long as I
could count how many pills were left in the
bottle, I knew what my wife was taking."

It was the kind of story she'd heard so
many times during her investigation, and
Skylar's mind flitted back to the conversation she'd had in Tyson's office two days ago
and how impassioned she'd been when she
told him about her case. The fact that drug
smugglers tried to take advantage of people
who were hooked on prescription drugs by
creating their own fake versions felt too evil
for words.

*Lord, please guide my investigation. We can't let evil win.*

Still her heart felt lighter. Filled with fresh hope and determination, she left the meeting, went back to her car and then drove to the Rocky Mountain K-9 Unit. She thought about the night before and how they'd stayed late going over the files together. The hours had just seemed to slip away as she and Tyson had sat in comfortable silence analyzing evidence.

There'd been something almost perfect about it, before his car had exploded and it'd felt like everything had been turned upside down.

The sun had set while she was in her meeting and all seemed quiet and dark as she pulled into the Rocky Mountain K-9 Unit parking lot just before eight thirty. She parked beside the kennels, between the pale golden light of two lampposts.

She found the front door locked. Had Tyson forgotten their meeting? She was about to leave, when Tyson came jogging around the side of the building with Echo on a leash.

It was only then she realized she still hadn't turned her cell phone back on.

Tyson slowed his pace and she walked over to them. The smile that crossed his face was professional and polite and did nothing to hide the deep worry lines that creased his brows.

"Was I right that we were meeting at eight thirty?" she asked. "I'm sorry if you've tried to reach me," she said. "I've had my phone off for the past couple of hours."

"I can't remember the last time I turned my phone off for anything," Tyson said, almost to himself. But not like he was bothered by it, more like he was impressed. "I sent the whole team home by six tonight. It's been a trying time for all of us, and I don't need anyone getting burned out."

Okay, in that case did he want to cancel on reviewing files with her tonight?

"Once again, the security feed was no help," Tyson went on before she could ask, "so I don't know where the bomb was placed in my car. But we got the results from the crime scene investigators. It looks like whoever set the bomb used ammonium nitrate and gasoline. But investigators also found traces of what looked like sugar."

"Sugar?" She felt her eyebrows rise. "Like they tried to put sugar in your gas tank and then blow your car up?" It didn't make any sense. "That's like poking you in the eye before shooting you. As for the other components, you can get ammonium nitrate from fertilizer and gas from any filling station, so my hunch is that we're looking at a homemade bomb assembled by an amateur who pulled the recipe off the internet. Which means someone who doesn't have access to more elite explosive devices, like active law enforcement or military, or someone who has the money and connections to get something which isn't homemade."

He took a step back and blinked.

"That was the forensic team's analysis too," he said. "You know your bombs?"

He looked genuinely curious and impressed, as if what she'd said had temporarily knocked his brain off whatever worried path it had been on. Once again, she found herself wondering why he hadn't invited her into the building and they were chatting in a parking lot. Could he have possibly been as thrown by their fleeting hug as she was?

"Yeah," she said. "I've always been interested in explosive devices. For a while I considered a career in explosive ordnance disposal."

"So you wanted to join the bomb squad," he said. "Military or police?"

"Police," she said. "I actually took electrical engineering as sort of a fallback degree in case my hopes for a career in law enforcement didn't work out."

His dark eyes widened. "You took electronic engineering as a backup," he repeated, dragging out the last word.

"Yeah," she said again, feeling heat rise to her face. "I've always been interested in figuring out how things work, which is why if you had been accepting new applications for the K-9 unit I was going to request a role in explosives detection."

With that the faint light she'd seen begin to glimmer in his eyes dimmed again.

"What they don't know is whether the bomb was on a timer or if they'd rigged my remote starter to act as detonation," he went on, and she had the feeling he was building up to something. "They assume it was triggered by my starter, because of when it went off, but can't know for certain. Both options are terrifying in their own way. If it's on a timer, I would've been stuck in traffic when it went off. If it was rigged to my remote starter and I'd left earlier when things were busier here, who knows how many people could've been taken out with me. It's also possible the bomb malfunctioned, and he intended it to do something else entirely. What we do know, from the security feed, is that the explosive device wasn't installed in my vehicle here. The criminal probably got to my car earlier in the day, when I was parked at the trails taking Echo for a morning run or even outside my house. Who knows how many hours I was driving around with a bomb hidden inside my car."

She sucked in a painful breath. "Which is even more evidence that whoever we're up against has been watching you."

"Right," he said. "Clearly I have a target on my back, and I can't justify extending that to anyone else. Now, I want to make it clear I appreciate everything you've done and brought to the table in terms of this case. Your professionalism, thoroughness and instincts are top-notch."

Okay, and where exactly was he going with this?

"But," Tyson said, dropping the single-syllable word with a weight that seemed to thud in the air between them, "as long as you're near me you're caught in the same crosshairs that I am. I'm happy to provide remote assistance on your drug case if and when I'm able, but think it's best if we don't meet up in person and you distance yourself from what's going on at the Rocky Mountain K-9 Unit. I'm worried the fact we went for pizza two nights ago and stayed late reviewing files last night might give the criminal the wrong idea, and I can't have you putting your life in danger by your proximity to me."

Oh. His tone was kind, gentle even, and something about that grated her. She was a proud member of the Denver Police Department. She didn't need this man, or anyone, treating her like she was fragile.

"Need I remind you that I came to you for help with a drug case?" she said. She didn't try to hide the bite in her voice. "Also that we can't rule out the possibility that the threats against your life and the drug smuggling case I'm investigating are linked. Every time I put on my uniform and step out the door to do my job I know I'm putting my life in danger."

"I know," Tyson said, "and I respect that. Deeply. But that's not what I'm talking about here. This is different. I'm not comfortable asking you to put your life on the line to help me."

"Why?" she asked. Did he think there was something wrong with her? That she wasn't strong enough or capable enough to handle this work? "How is it different that my asking you for help on my case?"

His eyes met hers, dark, fathomless and inscrutable. "It just is."

She felt her eyes roll and barely managed to turn away before he noticed. She turned and walked back to her car.

"Well, I can hardly force someone to work with me on a case," she said, "and I don't actually want to. So, I'm going to go get the box of files I brought. You can review them at your leisure and get back to me if you find anything helpful. Don't worry about returning them. I have copies."

She heard him say what sounded like "Thank you" but didn't look back, telling herself the disappointment in her chest was actually probably just fatigue from too many long days and short nights.

She reached her trunk and popped it open. Echo barked out a loud and sharp warning. She froze, feeling all the color drain from her face. A small explosive device lay in the trunk. It was another fertilizer bomb by the looks of it, smaller than the last one and tethered to a cell phone timer, which she suspected had been activated when she opened the trunk.

She had thirty seconds.

"Skylar!" Tyson shouted. "What's wrong?"

"Stay back!" she shouted. "It's rigged to explode!"

Nothing made sense about it. Whoever had planted this had no way of knowing she'd have been coming here. Did they plan for it to explode in front of the support group meeting? Why give her a timer? So she could warn people and make sure there'd be maximum chaos and witnesses?

Thankfully she and Tyson were the only ones there. But if she didn't do something fast it would take out the wall of the kennels and the two precious puppies she'd seen inside. Thick red drops of liquid dripped down from inside the trunk onto the explosive below. Her eyes followed the trail to the inside of her hood where a single word had been painted in what looked like blood:

BOOM.

# FIVE

Twenty-eight seconds to detonation. If she closed the trunk and ran away, she'd probably make it, but the explosion could collapse the training center wall and risk the lives of the dogs inside. She scanned the scene. Then her eyes locked on a large metal Dumpster over by the road. Its lid was open.

Echo barked louder.

Tyson was calling her name as he ran across the pavement.

"Stay back!" She raised both hands. "We've got barely twenty-five seconds before this blows."

Which meant she didn't have time to disarm it, only contain it. She glanced his way and met his eyes for a moment. Anguish filled his face and she realized with a jolt just how desperately he wanted to run to her rescue.

"Please, Skylar," he pleaded. "You've got to get out of there before it explodes."

"I'm going to do something, and I need you to stay back, in case it doesn't work," she said. "Very quickly, here are the details if I don't—" She swallowed. "It's a homemade fertilizer bomb, smaller than the last one, with a cell phone detonator. He's smeared the word *boom* in what looks like blood inside the hood, which is a clear escalation considering the last warning was in spray paint."

"Skylar—"

"Tell me you've got all that." Her voice rose. "Because if I don't make it, I'm counting on you to catch this guy."

"I got it," he said. Determination pushed through the emotion that seemed to strangle his voice in his throat.

"Good."

*Lord, help me now.*

She reached down, picked up the bomb and held it in both hands. It was lighter than she'd have expected and the wires weren't fastened as tightly as she knew they should've been. She hoped it would stay intact and inert long enough to get it away from the kennels.

"What are you doing?" Tyson shouted. "Put the bomb down!"

She steeled her breath, cradled the bomb to her chest and pelted across the pavement toward the Dumpster. Echo howled. Then she planted her feet and threw the bomb like a softball. She watched, as if in slow motion, as the explosive device arched through the air. It missed the opening and hit the Dumpster's open lid. Then it ricocheted off and tumbled into the Dumpster's metal depths. The lid slammed shut on top of it, she heard the sound of Tyson running across the parking lot toward her, then the Dumpster exploded.

A loud and metallic boom shook the air and seemed to reverberate around them. The Dumpster jumped six feet off the ground. The lid flew open. Flames and smoke billowed through.

She lost her footing and stumbled back. Then felt Tyson catch her in his arms and hold her to his chest. He guided her to the ground and they crouched there together, with his body sheltering hers, as flaming garbage rained down around them. The last scrap of burning paper fluttered to the ground in front of them where it sizzled out on the pavement. Tyson took her hands and slowly helped her to her feet. They stood there with her hands inside his and his gaze on her face. For a long moment, she stayed there, searching his eyes as if lost in watching the emotions flickering through their dark depths.

"Don't you ever—" Tyson started. But only three words slipped his lips before he caught himself and started again. "What were you thinking?"

"That if I ran and the bomb detonated in my car while it was parked next to the kennel walls, it might put Chase and Shiloh in danger," she said.

He closed his eyes for a long moment as if he didn't want to risk her seeing the feelings that were flooding them. He opened them again and pulled his hands from hers. His touch gently moved up to her shoulders. But his fingertips barely brushed her shoulder blades before he pulled back and crossed his arms again.

"Well, maybe it's a good thing you don't work for me," he said, "because I don't know whether to hug you, reprimand you or give you a medal for valor."

Then suddenly it was like the outside world caught up with her senses again. She heard the sound of shouting and turned to see the security guard running across the parking lot toward them. Tyson ran toward the man, told him to go back inside and that Tyson would be calling it in. Then Skylar realized Echo was still barking furiously. But not in the direction of the explosion. The dog's focus was fully locked on her car.

She turned to Tyson.

"Do you think Echo senses something?" she asked.

"Definitely," Tyson said.

"I thought he only detects drugs."

"Generally," Tyson said. "Echo did bark when you popped your trunk, so it's possible the explosive device had drug residue on it. Or there could be something else. Echo is a very unusual dog. This wouldn't be the first time he surprised me."

He stepped back, pulled out his phone and dialed. "Looks like I called it a day and sent everyone home too soon. We need to get an explosives detection dog down here."

Gavin Walker had the shoulders of a football lineman and a solid, confident way of walking into crime scenes that made everyone else around him feel as though they were in good hands. The RMKU's newest, and maybe final, hire had taken the open spot Daniella Vargas had left when she'd departed the unit to marry wilderness lodge owner Sam Kavanaugh and be a mother to his young son, Oliver. Gavin was another former member of Tyson's army ranger unit and had worked with the New Mexico State Police K-9 Unit before Tyson had recruited him. His K-9 partner, Koda, was a tall black-and-tan Malinois that seemed to fit Gavin to a tee.

When Tyson reached him on the phone, he was clearly in his car with Koda on his way somewhere, but he turned around in an instant and told Tyson he'd be there in ten. He made it in less than eight.

The K-9 building had been cleared and the security guard had created a police tape cordon around the parking lot. Crime scene investigators wouldn't be able to start processing the scene until Gavin and Koda confirmed there were no secondary explosives. Gavin parked on the street, opened the door for Koda to jump out, then strode up to the police tape. Gavin carefully stepped over it, Koda leaping beside him, and they crossed the pavement toward him.

Skylar had coordinated with emergency services, and told Tyson she was also making calls to the business owners in the area where she'd parked, in case they had any security footage. Maybe one of them had picked up something.

Echo had stopped barking, but still Tyson's partner radiated an intensity as if he sensed something and was frustrated that Tyson kept telling him to wait and wasn't about to let him go for it.

Tyson and Gavin exchanged greetings, and then Tyson stood back with Echo, while Gavin and Koda investigated Skylar's car and the surrounding area. But after a long, thorough and meticulous search, Gavin and Koda returned in agreement that the only explosive residue they detected was around the smoldering remains of the Dumpster fire. Skylar's car was clean.

"All clear," Gavin said. "Whatever's got Echo all riled up, it's not about to explode."

Tyson glanced at Echo. "All right, your turn, show me what you've got."

Echo barked sharply with a tone that sounded like the dog was saying "Finally!" Then the shepherd made a beeline for Skylar's trunk, sat in front of it and barked loudly. Tyson pulled on a pair of gloves, ran his finger around the inside of the trunk handle and found a faint white powder.

"We've got what looks like pill residue," he

said. "My suspicion is that whoever planted this bomb had handled drugs recently," he said. He pulled off the gloves, being careful to turn them inside out so that none of the evidence was lost. Then he glanced down at his partner.

"Well done, Echo," he said. "Good dog."

Skylar ended her call and walked over. "Find anything else?"

"Nope, we're all clear," Tyson said. Then he turned to Gavin.

"Skylar Morgan, meet Gavin Walker and his partner, Koda," Tyson said. "Gavin, Skylar is a detective with the Denver PD who I'm working with on a major drug case. There's a cartel that's smuggling fake prescription drug pills in through the Rockies, which are flooding the streets and putting countless lives at risk. She's also helping me crack who's been sabotaging the K-9 unit. Skylar, Gavin and Koda are our resident explosives detection team."

He winced internally for two reasons. Hadn't he just told Skylar they *couldn't* work together? And then when he mentioned Gavin and Koda's specialty, considering that Skylar had told him that explosives detection was her dream... But if any of that crossed Skylar's mind, not one iota showed on her face.

"Nice to meet you," she said. She stretched out her hand and shook Gavin's, with a smile both genuine and professional. "I've always been intrigued by explosive ordnance detection and disposal." She laughed self-consciously under her breath. "I hope that doesn't sound weird. I'd love to pick your brain sometime about getting into a K-9 unit somewhere."

A K-9 unit *somewhere*, Tyson noted. He'd figured she'd stick with the Denver PD if there wasn't an opening with the RMKU. That's when he realized that if he didn't convince SAC Bridges to keep the unit running, Skylar would just go ahead and apply for K-9 units elsewhere. Maybe even out of state.

Gavin crossed his arms. His grin widened and echoed in the bright blue of his eyes.

"Anytime," he said. "Always happy to talk explosives."

An unsettled feeling gnawed inside Tyson's core. He couldn't tell if he was sad at the prospect of her moving away from Denver or jealous to see a talented and handsome man get an inkling of just how impressive Skylar was. He had no reason to feel either. Skylar was a beautiful person, inside and out. It radiated from her. He could hardly be surprised if other people saw that. Not to mention that she was an incredibly good cop who was driven to achieve her goals. Of course she wouldn't let her inability to get a position within his unit hold her back.

"So, you used to serve together in the army rangers?" Skylar asked, turning her gaze so the question seemed to encompass both of them.

"Yup," Tyson said. "When you find someone solid who you can rely on, you want that guy on your team."

"Ditto when it comes to finding someone you'd trust to lead you into danger," Gavin said. His smile dimmed slightly at the edges, as if troubled by a memory that had just crossed his mind. "When we all got back from the other side of the world Tyson went out of his way to keep in touch with us, and make sure we were okay. No matter where we were or what we were doing, he'd send Christmas and birthday messages like clockwork. If one of our former brothers was struggling with something, he'd let us all know so we could pray or reach out and help. We'd do anything for this guy here." Gavin thumped a hand on Tyson's shoulder. "He's like the best leader, sergeant and cheesy older brother rolled into one."

Tyson felt his eyebrows rise.

"Cheesy?" Skylar asked. A smile crossed her lips.

"Oh yeah," Gavin said with a chuckle. "It's like every time we went out on operations he felt the need to say something inspirational, which was great, but he always ended up sounding like a Little League baseball coach."

It was nice to see the sadness that had filled Gavin's eyes just moments earlier replaced with joy.

"Like what?" Skylar said.

Tyson crossed his arms. "Go ahead, I can take it."

"He'd say things like 'Last one over the wall is a rotten egg!' or 'My only two rules are you gotta run before the bang and nobody dies today' or 'Remember a ton of bricks is only a thousand pounds!'"

"Two thousand pounds," Tyson corrected.

He laughed. So did Gavin and Skylar. Then the three humans and two dogs glanced at the trunk for a long moment.

"So, what do we make of the fact he's escalated from using spray paint for the first message to this?" Tyson asked.

"For what it's worth, I don't think that goop spelling out *boom* is blood," Gavin said. "It's way too thick and the viscosity's off."

"Well, it's easy enough to find out," Skylar said. "I've got a bottle of phenolphthalein in my first aid kit." She walked over to her car, got it out and slid on a pair of rubber gloves. Then leaned into the trunk with a cotton swab and carefully caught a splotch of red as it dripped off the *M*. "Now I add a drop of good old hydrogen peroxide," she narrated as she went, "and we wait. If it's blood within seconds the whole thing will go bright pink."

The three of them stood around and stared at it intently for over a minute. Nothing happened.

Skylar smiled and he could almost see the relief rolling off her shoulders.

"So it's not blood," Tyson said.

He turned to Gavin and was surprised to see the depth of relief in his eyes.

Tyson held his finger out, caught a drip of red and smelled it. It was sweet.

"Smells like sugar," he said. "It's corn syrup and food coloring, fake blood 101."

"So, more evidence we're dealing with an amateur," Skylar said. "First he spray-paints giant letters with the kind of paint you could get from any hardware store. Then this guy tries to make his own blood instead of buying prop or animal blood."

"Now, here's an interesting question," Tyson said. "The crime scene investigators detected some kind of burned sugar in the remains of my SUV. Did whoever's behind this write a message in my vehicle and it burned up before we saw it?"

"In which case, maybe that's why the explosive in my car was smaller and had a thirty-second timer," Skylar said. "Maybe our arsonist is still figuring out how to make explosives. I wondered if he'd intended it to go off when I was parked on the street, in which case the timer would've given people a lot of time to react and panic."

"And increased the likelihood of witnesses who were far enough away to survive the blast," Tyson added. "So maybe we missed another sugar message last night that burned up before we saw it and this is a second attempt to send the same message they tried to send last night."

"I think we're dealing with a real amateur here," Skylar said. "My gut tells me that whoever set the actual bomb is new to all of this and making it up as they go along. There's no real plan here."

"Which could fit with our theory that the man with the limp is working for the drug kingpin," Tyson said. "Maybe this kingpin is giving him orders and he's making a dog's breakfast of it."

Her eyebrow quirked. "A dog's breakfast?"

"Making a total mess of it," Tyson said.

Gavin's eyes glanced back and forth between them and his arms were crossed as if he was watching an impressive tennis match.

Tyson ran his hand over the back of his neck and prayed silently.

*God, please help us get to the bottom of this before anyone else gets hurt.*

Skylar's phone buzzed. She stepped back and glanced at the screen. Then he saw her whisper a prayer of thanksgiving under her breath.

"That's the owner of the convenience store that's kitty-corner from where I parked my car," she said. "He's emailing me his security camera feed. We might just have our first solid lead."

# SIX

Fifteen minutes later, Skylar and Tyson sat side by side in his office, reviewing security footage on his laptop. Gavin and Koda had left, crime scene investigators were processing outside his unit for the third time in three days and Echo was lying in his crate in what seemed to be his usual position with his paws sticking out the door and his snout lying on top of them.

Thankfully not only had the convenience store owner offered to send her his security camera footage without a warrant, but he'd also gone next door, talked to the owner of the Mexican family restaurant and gotten them to send their footage too. Skylar thanked God for them both.

Even with two different security camera angles, they didn't have the clear view of her car that Skylar would've hoped for, partly because it was obscured for several minutes by a delivery truck. But still it was enough to catch a few glimpses of a skinny man, swamped in an oversize hoodie, stepping toward the trunk of her car with a large backpack in his hands.

"Look familiar?" Tyson asked.

"If I'm not mistaken, he's the same man I saw taking our picture in the park Monday night while we were eating pizza," she said.

"Agreed," Tyson said. He leaned toward the screen and his arm brushed hers as he clicked another file on the computer. He sat back, and they watched the footage of the back of the K-9 training center and a familiar man in a large hoodie hop the fence. "Same guy?"

"Same guy," she agreed. "Also notice the limp?"

He nodded. "But he's moving so quickly my guess is that's not a recent injury."

Their working hypothesis was still that they had two perps to worry about. There was the unknown person who'd been running the large-scale drug operation, they assumed from jail, who they also thought was coordinating the attacks against Tyson and the RMKU. Then there was his minion—a skinny man with a limp and hooded sweatshirt—who had been painting walls, planting explosive devices, taking their picture and surveilling them. It was still just a theory, but so far it seemed to fit the facts at hand. She quickly ran everything she was thinking over with Tyson, who agreed.

"I also feel like once we figure out what the relationship and connection is between the henchman who's committing the crimes and the kingpin who's coordinating these attacks, we'll have a very large piece of the puzzle," she said.

He blinked.

"You think there's something larger at play here than just a lower-level bad guy who's working for a much bigger baddie?" he asked.

"Maybe," she said. "At the end of the day criminals are still people and that means they make decisions based on things like who they know, what they want and what they need, just like the rest of us."

She leaned back in her chair, closed her eyes and prayed for the perp who they assumed was the drug dealer's right-hand man. Had the limping thug gotten hooked on prescription drugs because of an injury? Was that how the kingpin had gotten his hooks in him and coerced him into running his operation for him while he himself was in prison?

Who was this man? What had led him to this?

*Lord, help us catch him before he hurts himself or anyone else.*

"So, the perp planted the bomb in your car when you were parked on the street," Tyson said. "What we don't know is if that was because he intended the bomb to go off there or if he'd been trailing you and thought that was the best opportunity he had to tamper with your vehicle. You told me you had a meeting tonight and I'm guessing it was in that area. Was it something scheduled? Would he have any reason to know you'd be there?"

She kept her eyes closed for a long moment. Just how ready was she to open her life up to this man? Then she opened her eyes and focused on the wall calendar opposite her and its red-*X* reminder that the big meeting with SAC Bridges about the future of his unit was happening in just two days' time.

"I trust you'll keep this confidential," she said. "But the church across the street from the strip mall holds a weekly Wednesday-night support group meeting for the friends and family members of addicts. I do go every week, so it's possible he followed me there. But he might've been there for his own reasons, recognized me and taken the opportunity that seeing my car there presented him. Dealers do tend to case support groups of all types."

"Even meetings for the friends and family members of addicts?" he asked.

She nodded. "Yes, partly because addictions tend to run in families, so the people attending might be vulnerable to that, and some will be former addicts themselves. But also because dealers are like predators who like to get their claws in people when they're down."

Although she'd tried to keep her tone professional and measured, she couldn't fully disguise the disgust in her voice.

"I'm sorry. It just angers me so much," she said. "Before I took this job I thought addicts had to actively go looking for drug dealers. I thought users sought them out, by meeting them under a bridge, or cruising some shady part of town, or going to disreputable clubs. But now I know that in real life there are probably dealers loitering right now outside of schools, hospitals, rehab centers and churches—the very places people go looking for help."

Tyson reached for her. His fingers brushed her palm as if he very much wanted to take her hand, and she was surprised at how much comfort she found in his touch. But then just as quickly he pulled away and crossed his arms.

"I imagine the fact you have so much compassion makes you very good at your job," he said. His voice was gruff as if battling to keep his own emotions in check. "Never apologize for caring about the people you serve and protect, okay? In my book, that's a good thing."

Somehow those were exactly the words that she needed to hear and yet they also made the tears behind her eyes grow thicker. She wiped them away with the palms of her hands.

"I take it you were at the church meeting following up on a lead?" he asked.

"No," she said and let out a long breath. "I was off duty and on my own time. I went for me."

His dark eyes widened slightly.

"I'm sorry," he said. "I didn't mean to pry into something personal."

"It's okay," she said.

Her gaze fixed on the wall opposite her and the beautiful patterns of red and brown in the brick. Something inside her wanted to open up to Tyson and let him get to know her better. And for her to get to know him better too.

"Growing up my parents were what you'd call *functional* addicts," she said, feeling her lips twisting over the irony of the label. "On the outside they looked like contributing members of society. I never saw my dad staggering around drunk or falling down. He always held a pretty well-paying and high-powered job, and according to the gushing family newsletter his current and third wife sends every Christmas, he still does. But he was angry all the time. He was very controlling and had to be right about everything. He'd sit and drink every night with this scowl on his face. And my mother would be constantly hovering around him like a panicked hummingbird, completely dependent on his approval and attention. Then he'd snap at her, and she'd cry and take pills." She shuddered and realized the tears she'd just wiped away weren't that far beneath the surface. "Sometimes he'd slap her or shake her and tell her that she was weak."

She heard Tyson suck in a hard breath.

"I'm so sorry," he said.

"Eventually neighbors called the cops on him," she went on with her eyes still fixed on the brick. "He stormed out, my mother begging him to stay, and never came back. It's been over ten years, and she still hasn't moved on. Every time I see her it's all she can talk about."

Skylar inhaled deeply, held her breath for a count of three, then blew it out as if exhaling the sadness of the memories.

"Going to the church support group reminds me that there's so much love, hope and faith in this world," she said. "I walk out so invigorated and determined to catch the very kind of criminals you and I are after right now."

It was only then she turned to look at him. As her eyes met his, the strength of the emotions she saw floating in their depths made a gasp rise to her lips. He was looking at her in a way no one ever had before. She saw compassion, respect and understanding all rolled into one, but deeper. Suddenly it was like every molecule in her body was aware of just how close the two of them were sitting and the gentle pressure of his knee touching hers.

The memory of the fleeting hug they'd shared in the car the night before filled her mind.

She wanted him to wrap his arms around her again, rest her head against his shoulder and let his strength envelop her. What's more, she knew something deep inside him wanted that too.

Instead he cleared his throat, pushed his chair back and stood.

"Thank you for trusting me with that," he said. Once again his voice sounded slightly strangled, like his throat was clogged with other words he was forcing himself not to say. "If SAC Bridges closes the RMKU down and you apply for K-9 units elsewhere, I'd be happy to do my utmost to help you with that. You're an incredible cop and learning this about you has only deepened that sense of respect. Hopefully we'll wrap this case up soon, catch these guys and be able to move. Now if you'll excuse me, I'm going to go check in with the crime scene investigators about your car now that we've confirmed it's not about to explode on you."

Then he turned stiffly and strode out of his own office, with Echo by his side, and Skylar followed, feeling as if they'd both left dozens of unspoken words littering the ground in their wake.

For the third day in a row, Tyson stood back, with his K-9 partner at his side, and watched as crime scene investigators went to work outside the RMKU. The irony would've been almost funny if the situation wasn't so serious. This time they moved through the scene much faster. After all, the only damage had been limited to the inside of one Dumpster and the bloodlike substance inside Skylar's trunk had turned out not to be blood. The car was swept for fingerprints, but the only ones found were

Skylar's. Seemed the man in the hoodie had been smart enough to wear gloves. Finding no substantial evidence, and after taking dozens of pictures, they released the car back to Skylar and told her she could drive it home. She retrieved the box of files she'd brought him from the trunk, which seemed no worse for wear despite having sat next to a bomb underneath a warning of corn syrup blood. Tyson relocated them to his office, telling her that he'd give her a shout if he found anything promising in them. And then for the second day in a row, Tyson found himself accepting a ride home from Skylar. This time it was in her civilian car instead of her official police car and he'd remembered to bring a doggie seat extension for Echo, so his K-9 partner could be buckled safely into the back seat.

She opened the back door for Echo, and the dog leaped in and pawed his way through what seemed to be two picnic blankets of different weights, two gym bags and a backpack. The faint scent of chlorine hung in the air, mingling with the scent of coffee. He glanced in the front seat and saw a huge coffee thermos and a giant water bottle. An even bigger water bottle lay on the floor behind the passenger seat, like someone had stuck a spout on a gallon water jug. The driver's-side door compartment was crammed to the brim with maps. And yet, despite being packed for adventure, the car was also remarkably clean and had clearly been well taken care of.

If cars had personalities, he definitely would've chosen to spend time with this one.

He watched as Skylar carefully relocated her back seat bags onto the floor to make more room for Echo.

Beside him in the driver's seat, Skylar fastened her seat belt, then looked at him funny.

"Your forehead is all wrinkled," she said, squishing her own forehead together with her fingers as if to demonstrate. "Why do you seem confused?"

He laughed. He'd never met anyone who could see right through him like she did.

"The front and back seats of your car look ready for a road trip," he said, hopping out to get Echo buckled into his seat, "but except for the files and explosive device your trunk was empty."

He remembered that when she'd gotten changed the night before last, she'd grabbed the big bag of clothes from the back seat of her vehicle and that it had looked full enough to last her a week.

"Huh." She chuckled under her breath and didn't answer, then once he was back in his seat, she pulled out of the parking lot.

"I never actually noticed that before," she said. "I think it's because I have a very busy life, I'm trying to live it to the fullest and I'm always in a hurry somewhere. So when I hop in the car I toss my swimming or gym bag over my shoulder and into the back seat and then fish it out of there when I need it again. Like I'm saving myself the step of running around to the trunk, unless I'm transporting something, like the files, I don't want to get squished."

He felt a smile cross his face and dozens more questions about Skylar filled his mind. But instead he held them back. He wished he'd said something better when she'd opened up to him about her parents. He wanted to tell her just how impressive she was and how deeply her story had impacted him. Had she also been reliving their hug from the night before in her mind? If so, did she think less of him for acting so unprofessionally? Was he the only one who wanted to have dinner together again and spend the evening going over the case and talking about their lives?

Truth be told, he didn't even know how to articulate the complicated feelings being around her stirred up in him. All he knew for certain was that he wanted to get to know her better but couldn't afford to spend the time to let that happen. He was in charge of the RMKU. He had just two days left to convince SAC Bridges not to shut them down. And even if he succeeded, he just didn't have the kind of life that lent itself to long walks and conversations with an interesting woman over take-out pizza.

No matter what his foolish emotions might think they wanted.

After twelve long and quiet minutes, she pulled up in front of the small bungalow where he and Echo lived. The street was quiet, although he noted with some surprise that a black pickup truck was parked in the driveway of the house that was under construction across the street.

He undid his seat belt and paused for a long moment, not knowing what to make of his impulse to hug her again like he had the night before. Instead he nodded curtly, hoping he didn't look as awkward as he felt.

"Thank you," he said. "I really appreciate the ride." *Appreciate* was a safe word to use, right? It was kind and respectful without being too much. "I'm going to be really busy over the next couple of days preparing for my meeting with SAC Bridges. But please do give me a call if you come across anything major. And I'll look at the files you brought over when I can and get back to you if I find anything."

"Sounds good," she said. "Good night."

"Good night."

He got out of the car, closed the door and had taken three steps before he realized he'd left Echo behind. He stopped and turned back to see Skylar reaching over into the back seat, unclipping Echo's seat belt and opening the back door. Echo bounced out and ran to his side.

"Good dog," he said and told himself the fact it looked like the dog was rolling his eyes at him was probably mostly his own imagination.

He heard Skylar slam the door and pull away. Tyson was halfway up his driveway before he realized that something felt wrong. He wasn't sure why. At first glance nothing seemed too obviously out of place. His lawn chair had fallen over, but that could've been the wind. His newspaper was in his black chokeberry bushes, but maybe the paperboy was just having a bad day.

Yet a sense of unease spread over him,

just the same as that sense of danger that had saved his life more than once on the battlefield. He placed his hand on the back of Echo's neck and felt an almost silent growl reverberate into the palm of his hands. Whatever was wrong, Echo sensed it too.

*Lord, whatever I'm sensing, please be by my side as my sword and shield.*

A red dot of light hovered on the dark wood of his front door.

"Echo, down!" Tyson shouted. He hit the deck, dropping flat on his face just as he heard the whiz of the sniper's bullet fly past him. A planter shattered, sending terra-cotta shrapnel flying around him. He rolled to his right toward the cover of a bristlecone pine. A second bullet flew and he heard the sound as it ricocheted against the brick wall of his house. He didn't see Echo anywhere.

*Lord, please protect my partner.*

He crouched up from behind the tree and looked out. Then relief flooded his core as he felt the warm and comforting bulk of the dog press against his side and realized Echo had made his way to him under the cover of the bushes. Smart dog.

Tires screeched and a car door slammed.

"Denver PD!" Skylar's voice filled the

darkness, ringing with authority. "Drop your weapon! Down on the ground!"

The bullets stopped. He looked to see Skylar running down the pavement toward the house that was under construction with her badge flying on a lanyard around her neck, and her weapon in her hands. The black pickup truck's headlights flared. The engine revved and the truck peeled off so quickly the tires screeched. Within a moment it was gone. Skylar turned and ran toward Tyson, shouting into her cell phone as she did so.

"Officer down! Send paramedics and backup. Shooter is on the loose. Black pickup truck, recently painted..."

He listened as she rattled off the directions to dispatch, describing the path the truck had taken and the details Denver PD's patrol needed to know to intercept and apprehend it. He stepped out from behind the tree with his hands raised slightly in what he hoped was a reassuring way.

"I'm okay," he said.

"And Echo?"

"Echo too," he said. "He didn't get us."

Relief flooded over her features. A look floated in her eyes that was filled with more affection than any hug he'd ever known. He watched as a silent prayer of thanksgiving to God crossed her lips. Then without missing a beat she raised her phone to her lips.

"Officer and K-9 are unharmed," she said. "Cancel paramedics. Focus all your attention on catching that truck."

She ended the call and turned back to Tyson. "You sure you guys are okay?"

"Absolutely," he said, oddly feeling the need to reassure her and make sure she was okay. "He only fired two shots. One took out a planter and the other chipped the brick. Do you think it was our guy with the hoodie?"

"Definitely," she said. "He got out of the truck to fire and then ran back to the truck when I turned my car around. He must've ditched the apple juice—colored truck."

"Or painted it black," he said.

She nodded and they turned and walked around the front lawn. A motion sensor floodlight flashed on above the garage and they saw the huge letters, in long streaks of red paint, still wet and running against the white garage door.

DIE.

Suddenly the three words the criminal had left so far rang like alarm bells in his mind.

*Run.*

*Boom.*
*Die.*

He knew those words, he'd said them before and suddenly he felt his legs go weak.

"He's escalated to death threats," Skylar said.

He reached for her arm and squeezed it.

"No," Tyson said. "I don't think that's it."

Her lips parted as if she wanted to say something more. But as her eyes met his she closed them again. He could tell she was waiting to hear what he was about to say, even as he could feel himself struggling for words.

"Gavin told you that I used to say cheesy things," he said, "to pep them up or cut the tension. He misquoted me before. What I used to say before we walked into really dangerous situations, the kind where I knew we might not make it out alive, was, 'There's only two rules. *Run* before it goes *boom*. And nobody's gonna *die* today.'"

He watched as the color drained from her face.

"I think the person who's behind all this and has been sabotaging the K-9 unit knows that and chose these words deliberately to mock me," he said. "Whoever's doing this is a former army ranger I used to serve with."

# SEVEN

At eight thirty Thursday morning, Tyson stood in his office, leaned back against his desk and faced three of the men on his team who he'd served with in the army rangers. To his left was Gavin, sitting by the window with Koda at his feet.

In the middle was Nelson, his light brown hair a little shaggier than Tyson would've felt brave enough to try for himself. Nelson had a healthy skepticism that helped him see through the kind of nonsense lesser men might've fallen for. His K-9 partner, Diesel, was a yellow Lab with the kind of friendly grin that belied just how talented the dog was. Nelson had recently gotten married to his wife, Mia, who he'd met on a tough case.

Finally, to his right was Ben with his tall and majestic Doberman partner, Shadow, who specialized in protection. Originally from Wyoming, Ben had recently married his wife, Jamie, and adopted her baby, Barbara June.

All three officers had been by his side in the thick of battle in Afghanistan and Tyson was hard-pressed to think of three men he trusted more.

It had been a couple of days since Skylar had first questioned why he'd tried to handle the sabotage of the RMKU mostly by himself and not brought the team in. He'd discussed the incidents with his officers, when they'd occurred and since, and they'd all compared notes, but Tyson had made it clear he'd take the lead on the sabotage, freeing them up for their own cases. When he'd wrapped things up with Skylar last night and said good-night, she'd pressed him on that again. And this time, under the circumstances, he'd known she was right. He didn't need to take this on without the backing and support of some of the best officers out there. He'd sent out a message to the three of them asking them to meet him in his office first thing that morning. Now here they were.

Echo lay in his usual place half in and half out of his open crate. Diesel lay on the floor beside him.

As the men shared a bit of small talk banter about their lives, Tyson realized that already he was battling the same urge to not burden his team. He took a deep breath, prayed for wisdom and imagined that Skylar was standing there in the room, with her intense green eyes on his face, keeping him accountable.

He started like he was briefing any other case. First he reviewed the training accident in April when Ben's K-9 partner was injured in a fall after a gun turned out to be overloaded with blanks. Next Tyson covered how he discovered the kennel's security keypad had been tampered with. He then moved on to the incident in June when several dogs got loose from the training center kennels, and finally the situation in August when the air-conditioning was cut off and several dogs got heat exhaustion. He recounted how he'd received an official warning from SAC Bridges last month and how worried he was about his final meeting with Bridges on Friday, when the FBI special agent would let him know whether or not he'd authorize their unit to continue.

He outlined in blunt detail everything that happened that week, being careful not to leave anything out. He then confessed that he knew he should've brought others in to help him with the case sooner, but that he'd wanted to free them up and handle it on his own. The entire unit knew about all the incidents, of course, from the first to the most recent, but Tyson had always let them know he had this, he'd deal with it.

Until now.

Finally, he explained how the three bright red words—*run, boom, die*—made him think that whoever was trying to take down the RMKU was someone they'd served with.

As he finished talking, he felt a heavy silence fill the room, weighed down with the unspoken words his three colleagues were debating whether or not to say. Questions and concerns filled their eyes, and he knew they were all thinking the same thing: How was it possible one of their own from the rangers could be responsible? Suddenly the face of their fallen colleague Dominic Young filled his mind. He remembered that moment, back in Afghanistan almost four years earlier, when Tyson had told these same men and others that he was going back into the terrorists' caves to rescue Echo. Dominic had volunteered to go with him.

If Tyson had refused his help and gone in alone, Dominic would still be alive today.

Tyson had never forgiven himself for that.

He watched as the men exchanged looks like an invisible hot potato, trying to decide who was going to speak first.

Ben leaned forward in his chair. "Who do you think it could be?"

Tyson felt a thick and sudden lump form in his throat. He swallowed hard. "I don't know. I hate that I even think it's a former ranger."

The three officers looked at one another— and then back at Tyson—and nodded.

"I'd like you each to make a list of the men we served alongside," Tyson said, "where they are now and any thoughts you have on them. Anything you remember that jumps out at you."

"We should also think about anybody who might also have known about Tyson's battle cry, someone who has a reason to be against us," Gavin said. "Maybe one of us has an enemy that is coming after the team. We should each check our own backyards to make sure they're clean."

"You said you're looking into the criminal records of anyone who might have a grudge against you," Nelson added. "You've got people on this team from all over the country. We should cast a wider net and send out a message to the entire RMKU team, including Daniella, to see if they've got anyone in their pasts who might be behind this."

Heads nodded, and voices murmured in agreement.

"Thank you, guys," Tyson said. "This all sounds great. But if chasing this down starts to interfere with anything else we should be working on, you let me know."

"Let us all know," Nelson said, "so we can have each other's backs."

Relief rolled over Tyson's shoulders like a wave. He thanked God for his team.

A motion on his left dragged his attention to the door.

The tall and imposing form of Special Agent Michael Bridges was standing in the middle of the open-concept office talking to Tyson's assistant, Jodie Chen. Immediately Tyson stopped lounging against his desk and leaped to his feet. Nelson, Ben and Gavin followed suit. As if sensing motion, both Bridges and Jodie turned and looked his way. Wasn't their meeting supposed to be Friday? Nervously, Tyson glanced at the calendar as if double-checking he hadn't gotten the day of their meeting wrong.

"Thanks for everything, guys," he said.

"Let's wrap this up for now and catch up later."

Nelson, Ben, Gavin and their K-9 dogs filed out of his office. Tyson ran his hand down his pants and then walked out into the main room toward SAC Bridges as the FBI special agent strode toward him. Although only in his midthirties, Bridges carried the authority of someone almost twice his age with the grip of a man who spent an hour every morning in the gym. As always, he was impeccably dressed, today in a perfectly pressed blue suit and periwinkle tie. He reached Tyson and they shook hands firmly.

"Special Agent Bridges," Tyson said. "I wasn't expecting to see you today. I thought our meeting wasn't scheduled until tomorrow at noon."

And he suspected the special agent wasn't there to give him the good news that his new K-9 SUV had arrived.

"Under the circumstances I thought we should move up our meeting," SAC Bridges said. "Do you have a moment?"

"Absolutely," Tyson said.

They went into the office, Tyson shut the door and the men sat. Nerves tightened Tyson's chest. He glanced at Echo's crate and then realized his K-9 partner was out in the common area socializing with his K-9 friends. While Tyson still had full view of his partner through the big glass window and usually didn't mind if Echo stretched his legs a little as long as he stayed close, he would've appreciated the backup of having him near.

"I hope I didn't interrupt anything," the other man said with a frown.

"It's fine," Tyson said. "We were pretty much done. As you know there have been escalating threats against RMKU, Denver PD Officer Skylar Morgan and myself in the last few days. The messages that the criminal has left at the scene has led me to think that maybe the person behind these attacks is someone we served with in the army rangers. So, I asked them to assist in the investigation and help me come up with a list of potential suspects."

The frown lines in SAC Bridges's face grew deeper. If he looked concerned when he walked through the door of Tyson's office, now he looked downright worried.

"You've hired a lot of people you served with in the army rangers," SAC Bridges observed. "Four of them, right?"

"Correct," Tyson said. "Nelson Rivers, Ben Sawyer, Lucas Hudson and Gavin Walker."

SAC Bridges didn't answer for a moment.

"They're good people," Tyson added. "We have a really good team."

"To be honest with you, when I gave the go-ahead a year ago to establish a mobile K-9 unit under contract to the FBI to cover cases in the Rocky Mountains, I wasn't sure if we were biting off more than we could chew," SAC Bridges said. "I recognized that there was a need for a very diverse and flexible unit to assist various authorities on cases within the Rockies. And I had no doubt that you were the right person to head up the unit. But the RMKU covers such a huge area, with far-reaching terrain, and I was concerned about how you'd be able to manage something so wide-ranging and maintain group cohesion, especially when I grew to realize how many of the cases would involve K-9 officers and their partners off alone without regular backup from the broader team."

Tyson nodded. It was true. Both Ben Sawyer and Harlow Zane had taken on cases in Wyoming. Chris Fuller had tracked down an escaped convict in Montana, Lucas was in Montana now and Daniella Vargas had relocated to New Mexico after taking on a case there.

"When I authorized you to put this team to-gether on a trial basis, I didn't fully realize the challenges of managing a unit of this scope," SAC Bridges went on. "I have to admit I'm deeply concerned about your inability to catch the person behind the targeted attacks to the unit and the fact they're escalating."

"So am I," Tyson admitted. "But we have some solid leads and we're forging on ahead."

Again, why was SAC Bridges in his office now addressing this? Why not discuss this over the phone?

- "Your officers are obviously very dedicated to the unit and the work," SAC Bridges went on, "and you've found innovative and suc-cessful ways to manage some very challeng-ing cases."

"Thank you," Tyson said, cautiously.

He had the unsettling suspicion that SAC Bridges was leading the conversation some-where and Tyson was pretty sure he wouldn't like where he was going when he got there.

"But I think the evidence is in and it's pretty clear you've been spread too thin to run this unit effectively," SAC Bridges said. "Thankfully, you've only got two dogs in the kennels right now, and the only other major case RMKU is working, outside your investigation, is the attack on Kate Montgomery with the car fire and the abduction of baby Chloe Baker, who'd been with her. So, it shouldn't be too difficult to start diverting active cases to other units and finding reassignments for your K-9 officers."

"Hang on." Tyson nearly pushed himself to his feet before he caught himself and sat. "Are you shutting down the RMKU right now? Have you decided we're done? I thought you weren't making the final decision until Friday."

His eyes must've shifted to the calendar on the wall, because SAC Bridges turned and looked at Tyson's neat rows of *X*'s as if seeing them for the first time.

"You're right. I did," he said. Then he looked back at Tyson. "But under the circumstances and the fact there's been an active threat on your life, I thought it made more sense to get this burden off your shoulders as soon as possible."

"What if I manage to stop this criminal before our scheduled meeting tomorrow?" Tyson asked.

SAC Bridges blinked.

"Well, obviously that would be a wonderful development," he said. His voice was measured. "And it would go a long way to freeing you up to address some of my concerns about the overall running of the unit. But I do still have other concerns. I outlined them all in a letter."

He reached into his pocket, pulled out an envelope and laid it on the table. Tyson realized SAC Bridges had come prepared with a formal letter explaining why the unit was closing.

"Why don't you leave me with this list of your concerns," Tyson said. "I'll review it and come up with some concrete solutions to fix the problems you've raised and then we can have our scheduled meeting tomorrow and review the situation. If you still think the best course of action is to shut down the unit then, I'll understand. Just give me twenty-four hours. That's all I'm asking."

SAC Bridges paused for a long moment. Then he nodded and stood.

"Okay," he said. "I did promise you a year. All of my concerns about the unit are laid out in this letter and we can take it up tomorrow at noon. However, to be honest, I'm not expecting my mind to change between now and then. I think you should start preparing yourself for the unit to be closed."

Tyson reached for the envelope and tightened his fingers around it.

"Thank you," Tyson said. "I appreciate it."

SAC Bridges nodded awkwardly. The men said their goodbyes, and as Bridges left, Echo slid back in through the open door.

Tyson dropped back in a chair, feeling like a marionette puppet whose strings had just been cut. Echo walked over to him and laid his head on his knee. Tyson reached down and scratched Echo behind his ears.

"Well, we've gotten out of tighter spots than this, you and I," he told the dog, softly under his breath.

But would they make it through this time? And if not, what would happen to the K-9 officers and their partners who got left behind? His phone buzzed to tell him a text was coming in. He pulled his phone from his pocket and glanced at it. Skylar.

Got a lead about a major drug shipment stashed in Red Rocks Park. You and Echo free?

He exhaled a long breath, surprised to feel something like a smile turn at the corner of his lips.

Yeah, he texted back. We're in.

\* \* \*

Red Rocks Park was a 659-acre expanse, just half an hour outside Denver, that was popular with both tourists and locals, thanks to its incredible huge red sandstone outcrops, many of which had fantastical names like the Seat of Pluto and Creation Rock. It was a daring place to hide a drug shipment considering how much foot traffic the more well-known areas got. Then again, it was also somewhere where nobody would think twice at seeing someone walking out with a large backpack.

When Skylar arrived at the K-9 unit, she'd found Tyson waiting out front in blue jeans, a leather jacket and rugged boots, and Echo clad in his official K-9 harness. She negotiated her way through traffic, with Tyson beside her in the passenger seat and Echo buckled into the back seat behind her. Slowly the tall and dazzling buildings of Denver gave way to the beautiful red plains and rocks of the national historic landmark ahead. As they drove, Tyson was reading what looked like a letter. He'd had the same letter in his hand when she'd picked him up, and she could tell at a glance it was on official-looking letterhead. His brows were creased in worry and he must've read over it three or four times before she interrupted him.

"What's that?" she asked. Then immediately hoped the question wasn't too nosey.

"Believe it or not," he said, "it's a letter from FBI Special Agent in Charge Michael Bridges explaining in great detail all the reasons why he's decided it's for the best that we disband the Rocky Mountain K-9 Unit."

The worry that pierced her core must have shown on her face, because he immediately reached over and brushed her elbow with his hand, in a gesture that was both tender and reassuring.

"No, we're not quite shut down yet," Tyson said, quickly. "In fact I still have twenty-four hours to turn it all around. Full story from the top. I took your advice this morning and called Nelson, Ben and Gavin in for a meeting. I asked them to put together a list of everyone we served with, or who they might've told about my cheesy lines, where they are now and any thoughts they have on the former rangers and who might be behind all this."

She silently thanked God he'd taken that step and prayed it would yield results.

"While we were wrapping up, SAC Bridges

dropped by for an unscheduled visit," he said. "He was so concerned about the current situation he didn't want to wait and thought we should take action right away to wrap up the team, move active cases to other law enforcement agencies, start relocating team members to new units and then call it a day."

He let out a long sigh. Instinctively she reached for him and brushed her hand over his arm in a motion similar to how he'd touched hers just moments ago. Only this time his fingers reached for hers. Their hands linked for a long moment. Then they pulled apart and she put her hand back on the wheel.

"I asked him for twenty-four hours to crack this case," Tyson went on. "Thankfully he agreed to that and that also gives me time to review his concerns and try to address them."

Her mind flickered back to their first meeting on Monday and the row of red *X*'s on the calendar leading to the meeting tomorrow. He'd been straight with her that he couldn't afford to take too much time away from preparing for that meeting.

"So, he left me with this letter he wrote outlining his concerns about the team," Tyson said and held it up. "Mostly it boils down to the fact our team is so expansive he's worried about how I can manage in such a diverse area. I mean, our unit covers several states and in the past year we've tackled cases in New Mexico, Wyoming and Montana as well as Colorado. That this sabotage was going on under my nose for so many months and I didn't manage to put a stop to it has him convinced I'm stretched too thin, and that creating a unit that covers such a big area was a mistake. To be fair, some of the points in this letter are right on the nose and things I should be addressing. On others, it feels like he just doesn't understand my team."

He blew out another long breath. Her heart ached and she wished she knew the right thing to say. She had so much faith in him and in his team. Why couldn't SAC Bridges see it?

Skylar pulled off the highway and past the Red Rocks Amphitheatre. The Colorado landmark had been built around a natural rock formation and was a favorite venue for bands around the world. She passed the tourist area and main parking, and instead steered down a long access road.

"He meant well," Tyson added "That's the hard part…"

His voice trailed off.

"But he wants to shut down the K-9 unit you love and have poured your whole heart into," Skylar said.

"Yeah," Tyson said. "That exactly."

"For what it's worth," she said. "I believe in you and in your team. The work you do is amazing and I'm confident you'll find a way to make him see that."

He pressed his lips together and didn't answer for a long moment. "Thank you."

The road grew rougher beneath their tires. Majestic red clay formations rose around them like statues rising from the earth. She slowed the car to a crawl and double-checked the coordinates on her GPS.

"So, tell me about this lead we're chasing down," Tyson said.

She rolled her shoulders back and sat up straighter.

"There was an early-morning meeting of recovering addicts at a drop-in center downtown," she said. "Bright and early at 6:00 a.m. for all those who need to head off to work or school afterward. I went undercover, in torn jeans, a baseball cap, no makeup and my biggest sweatshirt and just hung around the front building as if I was battling my nerves and couldn't decide whether or not to go in. I kept an eye out for some of the same dodgy guys I'd seen hanging around the church meeting the night before. Sorry, shouldn't have said 'guys' because a fair number of dealers are women. Anyway, didn't take too long before this young kid I recognized, barely seventeen, came over and asked me if I wanted to buy some pills. So, I pulled out my badge."

"That's some impressive investigative tactics," he said.

"All in a day's work," she said. She chuckled sadly as she remembered how scared he looked.

"He was so scared he didn't even run, though a handful of his buddies did. Instead, he just froze and started swearing and panicking. I took him into the drop-in center, where a social worker said we could use one of their rooms. Kid's name was Bernie Parks. I told him he wasn't under arrest yet, and he could leave anytime. You know, the usual drill. I just wanted to talk. Thankfully, he wanted to talk. He told me that his girlfriend was pregnant, they wanted to get married and he needed money. His girl was clean now, because of the baby, but owed a bunch of money to this guy named J-Rock. So now this J-Rock had Bernie doing errands for him to pay off the debt. While we were talking he got a text on a burner phone from this J-Rock telling him to come to Red Rocks Park to pick up some cash and drugs. He sent Bernie GPS coordinates, which are what we're following now."

"J-Rock," Tyson interjected, almost thoughtfully.

"Know the guy?" she asked.

He paused a long moment and shook his head. "No, but the name's oddly familiar. I'll think on it and see if anything comes up. Hopefully I'll remember."

"No J-Rock came up in any of my searches," she said. "But criminals can be a bit flexible about which names they use with different people."

She pulled to a stop. Orange-and-brown rocks spread out around them punctuated by low and scrubby bushes. They'd come so far off the main road it was almost as if they'd made their own tracks.

"Bernie said he'd tell me anything I needed to know," she said. "He just begged me to help him get him, his girlfriend and new baby away from the J-Rock creep. He said J-Rock was in his late twenties, balding and skinny with a *limp*."

Tyson whistled softly.

"Wow."

"Bernie didn't know anything about him sadly," she went on. "Apparently J-Rock just called the kingpin 'the boss.' But one of the social workers got us some breakfast sandwiches and Bernie got chatty. He said that he'd been around J-Rock when he'd been drinking a few times and J-Rock loved to talk a big game about how angry he was at the boss and was going to fight him when he got out of prison."

"So, the boss was in prison," Tyson said, like he was mentally ticking off a checklist comparing what she was telling him to the theories they'd come up with.

"Yup," she said. "J-Rock would have to go all the way out to the prison to visit this guy to get his orders but could only see him once a month, and not even that often. Plus, get this—he said J-Rock was mad because the boss had this vendetta against a cop and had him running around doing all these stupid errands like breaking into a police unit, painting messages and teaching himself to build bombs—"

"And that cop sounds exactly like me," Tyson said. That J-Rock's "boss" was willing to kill Skylar to get to Tyson told her all she needed to know about how ruthless he was.

"Bernie didn't have all the facts straight," Skylar said, "but he most definitely meant you. In J-Rock's mind, the boss's vendetta against this cop was going to get himself killed or arrested. Bernie actually laughed at this part and asked who was stupid enough to break into a police unit or go after a cop."

"Or filled with enough hatred," Tyson said. He blew out a long breath. "It's so cunning when you think of it, getting J-Rock to do his dirty work for him instead of going after me himself, so that if J-Rock is caught or arrested, his hands are clean." He shook his head. "I wish I had a whiteboard in front of me, so I could draw a suspect tree. On the bottom we have this kid Bernie—"

"And probably dozens of other Bernies," Skylar added.

"Agreed," he said. "Maybe even a handful of J-Rocks." He drew an invisible line in the air from Bernie to J-Rock. "Then at the top we've got the kingpin, whoever he is, sitting in prison and wanting me dead."

"Not just dead," she said. "Punished. Ruined. He's trying to destroy your entire unit."

Tyson leaned back against the seat. "And it's very likely he's someone I served with."

"One final thing," she said. "Bernie thinks this boss got out of prison a couple of days ago. He's not sure exactly but his fear of this guy is part of what made him so eager to turn himself in."

"If I was this J-Rock character, I'd watch my back," Tyson said. "Both because he's been mouthing off against his boss and because his boss might want to tie up loose ends before J-Rock squawks on him."

If so, would he wait until J-Rock succeeded in killing Tyson? Or would he take over his vendetta himself?

"So where's Bernie now?" he asked.

"Still at the drop-in center," Skylar said. "I made the call not to arrest him but instead to treat him as an informant. One of the social workers promised to try to get his girlfriend into safe temporary housing, and told me privately she thinks Bernie might need rehab."

"What if he runs?" Tyson said. "We could lose our only lead."

"I decided to have faith in him," Skylar said. "I've seen enough people try to turn their lives around to know all things are possible." She opened the car door and stepped out into the dry mountain air.

"I like that about you," Tyson said.

"What?" She stopped and glanced back.

"I like the way you have faith in people and believe in them," he said. "It's a good quality to have and one of your best ones."

A flippant quip about all of her other qualities crossed her mind, like the way they usually bantered. But for once she held it back.

"Thanks. I like the way you lead your team," she said. "It takes a special kind of leader to head up a unit as ambitious as yours and it says a lot that your officers really believe in you. I wish there was a way to make SAC Bridges see that side of you that makes your team so special."

Tyson paused a long moment without answering. She shut the car door and turned her eyes to the vista of red rocks surrounding her. Tyson got out of the car, released Echo and clipped his leash onto his harness.

"Now what?" she asked.

"Now Echo gets to work," Tyson said.

Echo sat obediently. His eyes perked as Tyson waved the empty baggie that J-Rock had dropped the other night beneath Echo's nose and told him to find more. Echo barked sharply. Then the dog put his nose to the ground and started to search. She was amazed at how focused Echo was as he paced back and forth across the ground searching for invisible clues that were too faint for humans to sense.

Tyson followed behind him as Echo moved this way and that, chasing a scent one direction, then doubling back as if he'd lost it and needed to find it again, and letting out low and quiet barks under his breath as if the dog was talking to himself. They walked farther and farther into the park and along the rocky terrain and still the dog kept searching.

Ten minutes passed, then twenty and finally thirty, and still Echo and Tyson kept following the scent with a diligent and laser focus that showed none of the frustration she was feeling. Finally the dog's ears twitched. He barked loudly, Tyson unclipped his leash and Echo started to run. Tyson and Skylar jogged after him, and she had the sneaking suspicion the dog was somehow matching his pace to how quickly he knew the humans could run.

A large rock formation loomed ahead of them. It was the size of a large house and looked like a stand-alone red clay cliff that rose straight out of the ground. They drew nearer and she saw the thin fissure cut through the rock as if it had been stabbed by a giant invisible knife. Echo reached the entrance and barked again, as if waiting permission to go inside.

"Show me," Tyson said.

The dog slipped through. So did Tyson. Skylar followed. The space was so narrow they had to walk single file. The earthy smell of the clay walls surrounding them filled her nostrils.

Within moments darkness surrounded them, as they grew farther and farther away from the sun. Awkwardly, she reached for her flashlight, feeling her elbows scratch against the side of the wall. She switched it on and held it aloft lighting the way ahead. Then suddenly Tyson stopped so sharply she nearly bumped into him. The tunnel had ended. The three of them crowded into a small space barely the size of a swimming pool changeroom. Echo barked triumphantly. The sound echoed around them.

Skylar shone her flashlight around the bare rock. "Now what?" she asked.

Tyson crouched down and pulled on a pair of gloves.

"Now I dig," he said. "Can you hold a light for me?"

"Of course."

"Thanks." He turned to the wall. "Also if Echo starts trying to dig, please let me know right away so I can stop him. I get the desire dogs must have to start digging stuff up instead of waiting for their much slower humans to do it. It's the one part of his training he still forgets sometimes, but then again he started his training at least a year later than most. But we can't let him either hurt himself or risk destroying evidence."

She glanced down at Echo. The dog looked up at her innocently under tawny eyebrows.

"Look, I get it," she told the shepherd. "So, I won't dig if you don't."

Tyson snorted. Then he started to dig, scooping up handfuls of dirt and clay. Even at a glance she could tell the ground was much softer than she'd have expected in a place like this. Somebody else must've been digging here recently. A moment later she heard him whisper a prayer of thanksgiving and she looked to see the shiny black surface of a garbage bag.

He pulled it out and sat back on his heels. The package was not much larger than a small backpack. Chills ran down her arms and she fought to keep the flashlight beam straight.

Tyson opened it. Inside were two thick stacks of bills. Tyson ran his thumb down each stack in turn, to make sure they weren't hiding anything else inside them. She wouldn't have put it past the drug dealers to hide a tracking device or explosive dye pack inside the bills to dissuade thieves or even dealers who might want to help themselves.

"All clear and all hundreds," he said. "Unless we're dealing with counterfeit, this here is a good fifty grand."

He handed the bag to Skylar, reached deeper into the hole he'd dug and pulled out four large freezer bags of small white pills.

"Whoa." Skylar sucked in a breath.

They'd actually done it. When she'd walked into Tyson's office on Monday and asked him to help her, she'd hoped it would be possible that Echo would help her find a stash like this. But the hope it could happen hadn't prepared her for the shock of seeing it with her own two eyes.

Tyson stood. He was so close to her that his chest almost bumped against hers. She held the flashlight between them, then looked up at Tyson's face. Joy danced in the depths of his eyes and it was like she could feel it spilling out into her own core, where it exploded like fireworks.

"You're incredible," Tyson said.

"Me?" she said. "You and Echo are the ones that found the stash."

"You found the lead that got us here," he said. "And you did it by doing your job with more compassion and grace than a lot of people would've had under the circumstances. I couldn't have done this without you."

The space between them seemed to shrink. She was acutely aware of his breath brushing softly against her face.

Echo barked sharply. It was a warning. But of what? And where?

Tyson turned away from Skylar and pressed his hand against the back of his dog's neck.

"I think there's somebody out there," he whispered.

And the three of them were trapped like fish in a very narrow barrel.

Tyson slid the packages deep inside his leather jacket. Then he reached for his holster and pulled out his gun.

"Echo and I will head out first," he said.

"Okay," she said. As much as she hated putting the precious animal in the potential line of fire, she also knew that Echo was a brave officer who'd trained to face danger.

She pressed herself against the wall and held her breath as Tyson and Echo slid past. She put away her flashlight, then pulled her own gun from her holster, and held it by her side as she followed them single file out of the darkness and back into the light. The air grew brighter ahead of them. She watched as Tyson hesitated at the entrance and glanced at his partner.

"Have you got a scent for me?" he asked.

Echo woofed softly, his ears dropped slightly and she could tell whatever he sensed he hadn't picked up a new drug scent. Tyson looked out into the bright sun, then cautiously stepped out into the sunshine with Skylar just barely a step behind them.

Then suddenly Echo snarled. Tyson turned sharply to a ridge on the horizon.

There stood a figure. His outline was nothing but an indistinct silhouette against glaring sun. His width made her assume it was a man. But she couldn't know for sure and the length of his shadow tricked her eyes into seeing him as eight feet tall.

She raised her weapon. Echo barked. The man turned and ran. No limp, she noticed.

So this wasn't J-Rock. For a fleeting moment his long shadow on the ground made it look as if there were two of them, one above the ground and one running on it.

"Wait!" Tyson shouted. He dropped Echo's leash and ran, dashing up the slope toward the departing silhouette.

She ran after him with Echo outpacing her. Even before Tyson reached the top of the slope she heard the sound of an ATV engine revving. Tyson kept running. He reached the top, a few seconds ahead of her, then stopped, with Echo by his side. She caught up to them and looked out over the vista of red-and-orange rocks spreading out below them, leading to the silvery blue skyline of Denver skyscrapers on the horizon.

"Search," Tyson commanded Echo. The dog diligently sniffed the ground for a moment, but it was clear he couldn't find a drug scent. The figure, whoever he was, hadn't been carrying or using recently. And even if Echo had been trained to track people, there was no way they'd be able to catch up to him on an ATV. Within a moment Tyson's brain seemed to realize that too, because he called Echo back to his side.

"It's okay," he told Echo. "He's gone."

"Could that have been the drug kingpin?" Skylar asked, then looked more closely at Tyson. "The way you chased him down... Did you recognize him?"

"No," Tyson said. "At least I don't think so. I couldn't really see him. But for a moment something about his stance tricked my brain into thinking he was someone he can't possibly be."

"Who?" she asked.

"Army Ranger Dominic Young," Tyson said. He turned to face her and ran his hand through his hair, now dusty from the red clay they'd walked through. "And it can't be him. Because he died in a cave explosion on the other side of the world."

# EIGHT

A search of the area turned up no more evidence of the mysterious figure they'd seen. Skylar didn't question Tyson further about Dominic and for now he seemed lost deep in thought. She couldn't help but wonder if the man they'd seen had been the drug kingpin, freshly out of jail and checking up on his operation. If so, had he suspected that Bernie had turned information about the drop over to the police? Even if he hadn't, he would now. She called the drop-in center only to find out Bernie had already left to see his girlfriend. She both called and texted the cell phone number Bernie had given her and got no answer.

She prayed for the teenager's safety.

Finally, they hiked back to her car and got inside. Slowly she turned the car around in a wide circle until they were pointed back toward the city.

"I told you about Dominic the other night while we were getting pizza," Tyson said. "I don't remember everything I said."

"You told me that he loved Echo," she said, "and that he never made it back."

"Which is all true," Tyson said. "But there's a short version of the story and a long one. I told you that we met Echo in the building complex we were securing. We thought it was empty, then Echo came running out barking his head off and warning us that we were in danger." He glanced over his shoulder to the dog now sitting in the back seat. "He saved our lives."

Skylar turned her head to smile at Echo.

"We took him back to the base with us," he said. "But he didn't really stay. He was a pretty independent dog. He'd come and go, then one day he didn't come back and we thought we'd seen the last of him."

He paused as if remembering a particularly unpleasant memory.

"Few weeks later, a group of us were on a rescue mission in the mountains," he said. "Gavin, Nelson and Ben were there along with some others, including several rangers who'd never served under me before. It was a big operation. Now, the caves of Afghanistan are in some ways remarkably similar to the Rocky Mountains. There is a whole network, like a labyrinth, which we sometimes used to travel or hide in. We had intel that a local warlord had kidnapped a diplomat and was hiding him in the caves. We went in after him. It was a pretty dangerous mission. In fact, I'm pretty sure it's one of the times I dropped the flippant 'run, boom, die' line that I now wish I'd never said."

She reached for his hand, but this time his arms were so tightly crossed, it was like they'd turned to rock under the tension. She pulled back.

"We found Echo in one of the caves," he said. "The dog was injured and chained up, but it was definitely him. Once we'd extracted the diplomat safely, I told my men that I was going back in to rescue Echo. Dominic volunteered to go back in with me. But then these explosions started going off inside the cave and we got separated. Echo and I made it out alive. Dominic came so close, we could see him running toward us. But then there was this major explosion and we just watched the flames envelop him." He swallowed hard. "He didn't make it."

Silence filled the car again. Her vehicle rolled slowly down the service road.

"Forgive me for asking," Skylar said, "but you know I wouldn't be doing my job if I didn't ask if you're sure there isn't some way he survived?"

She said the words as gently as she could, but it didn't stop the sudden burst of upset that flashed in his eyes.

"You're wondering if we just left him there, injured and behind enemy lines on the other side of the world," Tyson said, bitterly. Then it was like he caught himself and his voice softened. "Absolutely not. Not only did we watch him die, Gavin and I collected his body and brought him back to camp. His identity was confirmed by the medic and coroner, not to mention our own eyes. Gavin really pulled through for us in that moment and just focused on the task at hand, but I could tell that deep down he was shaken by it. Then, a few months later, we all attended his funeral. In fact Gavin and I were pallbearers. And we watched them lower him into the ground. I've thought about him every day since. I think knowing he lost his life volunteering to help me is what's made me so reluctant to involve others in anything I thought I should be able to handle on my own, including this case."

Again he paused for a long moment.

"Then today you thought you saw him here in Colorado," she said.

He frowned. "But obviously I didn't," he said.

"I know," Skylar said, "but the fact that the fallen brother was on your mind at that exact moment is really interesting and could be important. I remember investigating a double homicide that had taken place in a mall parking lot. This one witness to the event couldn't remember anything. Then she called 911 at three in the morning because she thought she saw a bear in front of her house."

"A bear," Tyson repeated.

This time there was an uncharacteristic but unmistakable tinge of skepticism in his voice and she reminded herself not to take it personally.

"Turns out it was a very large dog," she went on. "She'd just imagined seeing a bear. Probably due to her anxiety stemming from the trauma of the homicide. But the killer we were on the lookout for had a bear tattoo on his arm. Something the witness had barely seen for a second that had somehow gotten lodged in their subconscious. It actually helped us solve the case. Maybe the fact you thought of Dominic in that moment meant something."

"Maybe," Tyson said, after a long moment. "Or it could just be that having Gavin join the team knocked some memories loose. Not to mention witnessing the explosion on Tuesday."

"Another question I hate to ask," Skylar said, "but how well do you know Gavin?"

"Well enough," Tyson said. "I know his heart. I've seen his faith, his courage and the mettle of what he's made of. I could tell he was pretty shaken up by what happened to Dominic. But I certainly don't think for a fraction of a second he could have anything to do with any of this."

"Okay, that's good enough for me," she said. "I trust you and you trust him."

"Thank you," Tyson said. His tightly crossed arms began to relax. "It means a lot to hear you say that."

"What about Dominic," she asked. "Any complicated family history? Drug or alcohol use? Was he ever in trouble with the law?"

"No, nothing like that at all," Tyson said. "He had a very strong sense of right and wrong. Deeply ingrained values, about devotion to his country and God. He told me once he'd debated becoming an army chaplain, actually. His funeral was mostly people he'd served with. Maybe an elderly relative or two. But he was an only child and both his parents died when he was eighteen."

"Any red flags at the funeral?" she said. "Any references to mistakes in his past?"

"No," Tyson said. "His funeral was glowing. Nobody had a bad word to say about him."

She felt her forehead wrinkle.

"I hear you," she said. "But in the real world nobody is actually perfect. We've all made mistakes or missteps."

"You think there's a metaphorical bear in Dominic's history that lodged in my subconscious which the man on the ridge reminded me of?" he asked.

"I don't know," she admitted. Her eyes rose to the road behind her. They were still in Red Rocks Park on a service road. Only now there was a black pickup truck behind them and it was closing fast.

"We've got company," she said. "Black pickup."

He turned and looked over his shoulder.

"Is it just me or does it look like the same

truck that tried to run us down on Monday and that we saw outside my house last night?" he asked.

She nodded. "Yup."

In the harsh light of day, it was even clearer to see the formerly apple juice–colored pickup had gotten a bad makeover.

"So different man, but same truck," he said.

"Looks like it." Her gaze darted to the rearview mirror then back to the road ahead. "Can't see his face. Just a hoodie."

"He's wearing some kind of mask," Tyson said. "Stocking, I think."

Fear brushed her spine. They were still deep in the park. Tall rocks rose from the plains on either side. There was nowhere to hide. Nowhere to run. She watched as Tyson unholstered his weapon.

"I'm calling it in," she said. "I can't make out the license plate. Can you?"

"No, he's got some kind of distortion filter over it."

She reached for the radio. But before her hand could touch it, she heard Tyson shout.

"Stay down! He's got a gun!"

Gunfire shook the air around them. A rush of air and shattered glass hit her back as the back window exploded. The vehicle spun.

\* \* \*

For a long and terrifying moment, the world flew past Tyson's eyes in a blur. Huge red rocks loomed in front of them. Skylar prayed loudly, calling out to God for help, as she battled the wheel. Then the vehicle flew off the road and down the slope.

They were going to crash.

His body lurched against his seat belt as they slammed to a stop. But not with the jarring thud he was expecting of the vehicle hitting a rock. No, this was more like the crunch of a soda pop can being bent under the weight of his thumb.

He looked out to see the front of the car was just inches away from a tall rock formation the size of a cement mixer and lodged into a thick outcropping of bushes. *Thank You, God!* He glanced to Skylar and saw her grab the radio and start calling in for help. Her hair had been tossed loose from its usual bun. Glass shards clung to the strands like snowflakes.

"Skylar, you okay?"

"Yeah, you?"

"Yeah."

"I think he's gone," she said.

Then he heard a small plaintive sound that shook him to his core.

Echo was whimpering.

Tyson glanced over the back seat. Echo sat stock-still in his seat belt, with his eyes and tail down and his body covered in broken glass. Blood dripped from a cut on his right front leg. Tyson's heart lurched.

"It's okay, buddy," he said gently. "It's going to be okay. I'm going to get you out of here."

He shoved his door open, hearing the high-pitched sound of bushes scraping the paint off the metal. Skylar was on the phone with emergency services now, but as he stepped out she paused.

"How's Echo?" Skylar asked.

Her skin was pale, and he could see the worry flooding her bright green eyes.

"He's cut," Tyson said. "But thankfully the seat belt kept him from being tossed around."

"Hand me the packages," she said. "I'll take over chain of custody for the evidence and coordinate with emergency services. You take care of him."

He gave her the packages, and she tucked them inside her jacket, shoved her door open with both hands and her leg and started to-ward the service road. He made his way through the bushes to Echo's door and opened it. The dog looked at him with sad and worried eyes.

"It's going to be okay," he said again.

Echo woofed softly.

Slowly and carefully he brushed the glass away from Echo's fur, starting with the top of his head and working his way down the dog's body. Echo leaned over and licked his hand as if to say thanks.

"You're welcome, buddy," he said. "But right now I need you to just sit still and keep your tongue in your mouth. I don't want you accidentally cutting it."

He cleaned the glass from the seat around Echo's paws and then turned to the gash on the dog's leg.

"Don't worry," he said. "It's not as bad as it looks. I'm just going to bandage it with some gauze from Skylar's first aid kit and then we'll get you to Dr. Jones. I'm sure she'll have you all stitched up and fixed in no time."

He got the first aid kit, bound the cut and only then did he carefully take Echo's seat belt off, pull the dog into his arms and lift him from the car. He started back toward the service road. Emergency lights and sirens rose to greet them. He felt Echo tuck his head into the crook of Tyson's neck.

When he reached the road he saw Skylar briefing a Denver PD officer, but he barely had time to nod in her direction before a couple of paramedics ran over to him and tried to usher both him and Echo toward an ambulance. It was only then he realized he had Echo's blood on his jacket.

"I'm okay," he said. "I'm not injured. Just my partner."

The paramedics exchanged a few words out of his earshot, then told him that as neither he nor Skylar were injured, they'd be heading back to the city and would be happy to drop him and Echo back at the RMKU. Gratefully he accepted the offer.

Once again, something inside him was pulling him to stay by Skylar's side, like a magnet buried deep inside his core. But she had a job to do and he had to focus on getting Echo the help that he needed.

He waved goodbye to Skylar, who mimed that she'd call him later, then he climbed into the back of the ambulance with his partner in his arms.

The drive to the RMKU was a blur of worry as he held his injured partner, despite the paramedics offering he could set the dog down on the stretcher. When he reached the

RMKU, he found the vet, Sydney Jones, standing outside waiting for them. Considering his arms had been full, he assumed either the paramedics or even Skylar had called to give her a heads-up.

Within moments, Sydney had Echo in her office, up on her operating table and sedated.

If he was honest, Tyson had never known exactly what to make of the unit's vet, who also had her own local veterinary practice in town. Her desk was lined with pictures of a veritable menagerie of animals, including a horse, a goat, a cat and a parrot, all of which he'd learned were her own pets. Her bedside manner was blunt and outspoken, like she cared more about advocating for her animal patients than worrying about what the humans thought of her. She'd taken care of Shadow when he'd been injured in the training accident in the spring and had been very cautious—some would say overly cautious—about clearing the dog to return to duty.

Tyson knew without a doubt that Echo could be in no better hands.

He watched and waited, bouncing with nerves while the vet stitched him up, until she presumably got tired of his jitters and she told him to get out of her operating room and wait in the hall. There he paced back and forth, like a parent waiting to find out if his kid was going to be okay.

Finally, she stepped out.

"Echo is fine," she said. "The cut was long but relatively shallow. I'd tell you to keep him off it, but being a dog he'll probably be trying to walk on it tomorrow. If he wants to do that it's up to him. But don't let him have any serious exercise for a few days. His stitches should dissolve on their own, but I'll check them again tomorrow after your meeting with SAC Bridges."

He couldn't remember telling her about the meeting, but it was on the calendar in his office and probably a hot topic for conversation about the RMKU.

"When can I bring him home?" he asked.

"Several hours at least," the vet said. "He'll have to sleep off the sedation and then I want to keep him under surveillance for a bit just until I'm sure he didn't suffer any other injuries in the accident we might've missed. I'll call you when he's ready to go."

"Thank you," he said.

"No problem." The vet turned back toward her office. Then she paused and looked back.

"I hope everything goes well with SAC Bridges," she added. "This is a wonderful unit and it's been a real privilege to work with these dogs."

Just as he'd figured, word of the meeting had likely spread to anyone who worked with the unit. They were all counting on him to keep the unit going. He couldn't let them down.

Tyson walked next door to headquarters and headed to his office. It was only then that he caught a glimpse of himself in the tall glass windows and saw the blood and dirt that streaked his clothes and that he still had glass in his hair. Thankfully he always kept a few changes of spare clothes in his office. He carefully combed the glass from his hair, cleaned himself up, changed into fresh clothes and headed for his desk.

There were three lists of people he'd served with overseas in his wire in-box from Nelson, Ben and Gavin. When he turned on his computer, he found that true to his word, Nelson had emailed the rest of the team to make lists of anyone with grudges against them and that Chris, Lucas and Harlow had sent in lists as well. So had Daniella, although she'd now left the team, and she'd gotten a few ideas from her ex-military husband, Sam, even though he'd never served with Tyson overseas.

He printed the emailed lists out and laid them on his desk beside the handwritten ones. His eyes glanced at Echo's crate. The office seemed oddly empty without his partner.

Tyson sighed and got to work. He pulled two large yellow pads of paper out of his desk. On the first he made a combined list of all the names, underlining any name or tidbit of information that seemed particularly interesting. A couple had had minor brushes with the law. Three had been in rehab programs for alcohol and pills including one who Ben noted was currently living in a halfway house in Denver.

Then he got out SAC Bridges's letter and wrote down each of his concerns on the top of a separate page on the other pad of paper. He made special note to copy Bridges's concerns exactly, word for word, so that he didn't cloud them with his own thoughts and feelings. Methodically Tyson made notes under each one, jotting down everything he agreed and disagreed with, including every practical suggestion he could think of to address them.

Despite the fatigue that had clung to him for months like a cloud he couldn't shake, he actually really enjoyed the paperwork side of being the head of the unit. He liked analyzing problems, overseeing the team and managing assignments. He just didn't like feeling it was all he did or thought about from the second he got up in the morning to the moment he fell asleep at night.

If the unit shut down, he knew he'd do his utmost to make sure his team was fine and found amazing new assignments. But after that, where would he end up? Would he ever find a job that he loved this much? Or a role that he felt so called to?

A knock drew his attention to the door. He looked up to see his assistant, Jodie, standing there. Short with shoulder-length black hair and huge glasses that made him think of a happy owl, Jodie had worked for him since the RMKU had opened its doors, and he was endlessly thankful for her. She was organized and hardworking in a way that never ceased to impress him, as well as having such a deep affection for the dogs in their care.

"Sorry to interrupt," she said. "But do you have a moment?"

He stood and waved her to the same chair opposite him where SAC Bridges had sat earlier that morning.

"Please," he said. "Come on in."

"I was sorry to hear about Echo," she said. Worry filled her eyes. "I passed Sydney in the hall and she told me he's doing well. Can I ask how your impromptu meeting with Michael Bridges went this morning?"

"He was ready to start shutting us down right there on the spot," Tyson admitted. Her dark eyes widened. "Thankfully I managed to get him to give me a list of his concerns and I have until tomorrow to come up with solutions." He held up the yellow pad. "Here's what I've got so far. Also, Skylar and I made some serious progress on her case today and I haven't given up hope that we'll catch the guy and very soon."

"Well, for what it's worth," she said, "I'd be happy to take a look at the list of his concerns and see if I have any suggestions as it relates to the administrative part of our unit. Might even be worth passing it around to a few people, or even the whole team, to see if they have any ideas. Second, third and fourth pair of eyes never hurt."

He nodded noncommittally and couldn't help but notice that sounded like something Skylar would say.

"I was actually coming to see you about

Shiloh," she added. She leaned forward in her chair. Jodie was the hearing child of a deaf mother, and her hands often moved as she spoke, as if she was instinctively translating for herself. "I know you've heard the black Lab isn't going to be assigned to a K-9 officer, right? He's sort of our first dropout of K-9 training school?"

He smiled wryly.

"I wouldn't quite put it like that," he said. "But yes, there's always a percentage of dogs who don't make it through these kinds of training programs. In Shiloh's case he's intelligent enough but he's just missing that ability to block the humans out around him."

"He's a very caring dog," Jodie said.

"Agreed," Tyson said. "If he was a person I'd tell him that maybe he wasn't cut out to be an army ranger but would make a great medic."

Jodie smiled broadly.

"I'm really happy to hear you say that," Jodie said and signed. "Because I've been spending some time with him, and I have an idea."

"Really?" Tyson leaned forward too, feeling his attention piqued. "What are you thinking?"

"I started noticing that whenever I was talking to Shiloh he would pay attention to my hands," she said. "After a while I tried just signing instead of talking and to my surprise he responded right away. Much faster than he reacted when I talked with my hands in my pockets."

"Wow," Tyson said. Yeah, he had heard that some dogs responded to physical cues better than verbal ones. They just weren't usually cut out for K-9 work where the ability to follow verbal commands or clickers was essential.

"As you know, my mother is deaf," Jodie went on. "I've been around hearing dogs my whole life. Shiloh is so smart, responsive and eager to learn. I was wondering if there was any way I could adopt him, take him home and train him as a service dog for the deaf and hearing impaired."

Tyson felt a smile cross his face. It was a brilliant idea, and one he'd never have thought of. Maybe he'd been wrong to try to do so much on his own without bringing the others in. Who knew what other out-of-the-box ideas were out there?

"That's a fantastic idea," he said. "Thank you for bringing it to me. Write me a quick email outlining what you've suggested, and I'll pass it on to SAC Bridges with my strongest recommendations. I can't promise what his responses will be, but I'm pretty hopeful he'll sign off on it."

Not to mention it would tie up one more loose end if the RMKU closed.

"Thank you," Jodie said. "I will."

She beamed. It was the same look of happiness and joy he'd seen in every person he'd ever partnered with a K-9, and one that he hoped he'd be able to see in the face of new recruits for many years to come. His cell phone began to ring before she could say anything more. He glanced down at the caller ID on his screen. It was Skylar.

"I'm sorry," he said. "I have to take this. But I'm excited about this opportunity for you, and you have my full support."

"Thank you," Jodie said again.

He waited until she stepped out of the room and then answered the call. "Skylar, hi!"

"Tyson," she said. Her voice was slightly breathless as if she'd been running. "How's Echo?"

"Echo's good," he said. "Cut's not too deep. Sydney got him all stitched up and resting. I'm just waiting for her to give me the go-ahead to take him home tonight. How are you?"

"There was a partial fingerprint on one of the packages," she said. The words nearly burst from her lips in a rush. "The analysis team processed it right away. The money's authentic too and the full fifty grand. The drugs are also the real deal. And even though it's only the sliver of a partial print, and so not enough yet to get an arrest warrant, we've already got a potential match in the system."

He leaned back in his chair and blew out a hard breath. "Let me hear it."

"Get this," she said. "It belongs to a former army ranger named Jason Roque."

"I served with him!" Tyson nearly shouted. No wonder the J-Rock moniker had been vaguely familiar. "Not closely, but he was part of the bigger team on the operation where Dominic Young was killed. I didn't catch it sooner, because he pronounced his name like *row* but with a *k* at the end."

He grabbed the yellow pad of names and started to flip through it.

"Any idea where he is now?" she asked. "His last known address is a couple of years old, and the house has been sold since."

"Actually I do," he said. Thanks to the fact

he'd taken her advice and gone to his colleagues for help. "According to Ben, he spent a six-month stint in rehab and now lives at a local halfway house."

"Pills?" Skylar asked.

Tyson checked the notepad.

"Yes, and alcohol."

"Was he injured on duty?" she asked.

"I don't know," Tyson admitted, "but it might explain the limp."

"And how he might've been vulnerable to getting addicted," Skylar said. "Is he still there now?"

"Don't know," Tyson said. "But there's only one way to find out."

He heard the sound of her chair creaking down the phone line as if Skylar was leaping to her feet.

"I'll be there to pick you up in fifteen minutes," she said.

"I'll be ready in ten."

# NINE

**W**hile he waited for Skyler to arrive, Tyson quickly checked in with the team to fill them in and see if any of them had a recent picture of Jason Roque or knew anything more about what had happened to his life since he'd left the military. Ben had heard about Jason's stint in rehab through a shared friend they had on social media. Jason's social media pages were inactive, but Ben was able to pull a picture off one site.

Jason was a thin man, with an oval face, receding hairline, limbs that seemed a little too long for his body and an eager smile. Tyson was pretty sure it was the same man who Bernie had called J-Rock, who they'd seen trailing them in the park and who had repeatedly threatened their lives.

Sadness filled Tyson's core. Gavin hadn't been exaggerating when he told Skylar how diligently Tyson had tried to keep reaching out to the people he'd served with. What Gavin hadn't known was just how many never responded or how often emails bounced.

What had started Jason down the path he was on? How had there been no one to help him? Could Tyson have done more? He prayed to God that it wasn't too late for Jason to turn his life around even if it would be from inside a prison.

Tyson checked in with the vet, who told him Echo was resting and reassured him she'd call when Echo was good to go. Then he stepped outside to find Skylar was dressed in civilian clothes again and waiting for him in her personal car.

"Good news is that my police vehicle still runs," Skylar said as she leaned over the seat and let him in. "Just needs to have some dings smoothed out and the bumper replaced. They've already issued me a new one, but considering we're going to a halfway house I thought it was better not to go in a police car. We don't want to scare off any potential witnesses."

He got in and closed the door.

"I hadn't realized just how thin we were stretched until I tried to get my hands on a new vehicle," he said. He buckled his seat belt and she started driving. He still wasn't expecting it until Monday. But the irony would be SAC Bridges shutting down the unit tomorrow and his new SUV arriving early just five minutes later. "I mean, I knew with Gavin it took a week for his SUV to come in. We didn't have any spares in the garage and vehicles like that have to be specially ordered from a dealership in another state. But, I had no idea what it would mean practically for an officer to be without a vehicle for this long."

He made a note to add that observation to the yellow notepad on his desk. They'd done so much in the space of a year. Members of his team had solved kidnappings, stopped killers, brought criminals to justice and saved lives.

But they had the potential to be even better. And the idea of that would've excited him if he wasn't worried he'd realized that too late.

He showed Skylar the picture of Jason that Ben had downloaded off the internet as they drove and filled her in on the limited information he'd been able to glean from the team about him. She was certain he was the man with the limp who she'd seen watching them in the park.

Skylar had brought with her a copy of his mug shot from a drug arrest and another from an assault charge. The two of them decided together that if they needed to show a picture around they'd go with Tyson's picture instead.

They reached the halfway house in less than twenty minutes. He didn't quite know what to expect, but it was a typical large house, with a big front lawn, in a suburban neighborhood. The only difference he noticed was that there was a low wall with a gate and garden beds growing vegetables on the lawn where he'd have expected to see bikes and baseballs.

"How many people live here?" he asked.

"Six is the maximum," she said. "They wouldn't confirm anything over the phone, due to an abundance of caution, even though I've been here on cases before. But that doesn't surprise me. A lot of people who stay in places like this have people in their past they need to get away from."

As they approached the house, he couldn't help but notice the thick but neat lines of black paint that crossed the wall in front of the house.

He nodded toward it. "I'm guessing someone painted over graffiti?"

"Yeah," Skylar said. "Hateful stuff. Not from the people who're here getting a second chance. But from those who don't want recovering addicts in their neighborhood."

He opened the gate, and they walked together up the long path. On the one hand it was hard to blame the residents for being worried about former addicts living nearby. But that didn't justify letting fear turn into hate. And it was also impossible to imagine getting clean without a safe place to do so, in a community where they could get jobs, visit with their family and friends, and even just walk safely down the street and smell the fresh air away from the dangers and temptations of the lives they'd left behind. He was relieved Jason had found such a place.

Skylar knocked on the door and stood back. They waited a beat before the door was opened by a man with a gray beard and bright blue eyes who Skylar introduced as the head social worker. Behind him Tyson watched as a beautiful orange-and-white cat darted up the stairs, past what looked like hand-painted artwork of green forests and mountain ranges.

Skylar showed the man Tyson's picture of Jason and explained that they wanted to talk to Jason about a serious drug case. The social worker told them that sadly Jason had been asked to leave six months ago when he was caught trying to sell pills to others in the house. Last he'd heard Jason was now living in his old trailer in the Rocky Mountains and he'd heard enough through the rumor mill to give them a solid idea of the area where he'd be parked.

Skylar and Tyson thanked him for his time, got back in the car and drove in silence to the Rocky Mountains. Tyson's mind was filled with thoughts of Echo, his team, Jason, his meeting with SAC Bridges tomorrow and all the concerns that had been raised in the letter. But Skylar didn't seem to be in any hurry to break the silence. He glanced her way hoping to catch her eye. Instead her gaze was locked on the road ahead. Her brows knit and a deep worry filled her eyes.

The buildings of Denver gave way to flat plains, then to steep slopes and finally thick trees. After searching the area, they found the trailer parked illegally on the outskirts of a disreputable campsite that was closed for the season. From the outside Tyson guessed the medium-sized trailer had one bedroom and a table that folded into a second bed. Brand-new, it had probably been worth a pretty penny, but now the paint was peeling and cardboard had been taped over the windows from the inside. There were no vehicles in sight and the door was locked with a padlock from the outside. They got out and looked around. Cigarette butts, needles and empty liquor bottles littered the ground.

"I'll take the trailer—you take the perimeter?" he suggested, thinking his height advantage might help him peek around the cardboard into the windows. She nodded and started taking pictures of the tire tracks and debris. He knocked on the door, not that he expected an answer but rather hoped very much there was no one locked inside. Then he listened but heard nothing but silence.

"I'm guessing just one person lives here," he said.

"Agreed," she said. "I'm only noticing one set of footprints. But look at this." He followed her voice to where she'd pointed at the grass. The first thing he saw were the red and black spray paint bottles. Then a scorched patch of earth, where it looked like something had been set on fire and then quickly put out.

"Whoever lives here painted his vehicle black recently," she said, "did something with red paint and set something on fire. I don't

know if it'll be enough, though, to get a judge
to issue me a search warrant, but I'll try."

He hoped so. His phone began to buzz
in his pocket. He reached in and pulled his
phone out. It was Sydney.

"Hello, Tyson here," he said.

"Good news," the vet said. "Echo is awake,
well rested and eagerly waiting to see you."

Skylar waited outside in her car as Tyson
went into the RMKU training center to get
Echo. A few minutes later he came out again,
carrying his partner in his arms. Something fluttered in her heart as she watched
the strong man with broad shoulders gently
carry the large dog toward her vehicle. Echo's
head rested on Tyson's shoulder. A white
bandage was wrapped around his right leg.
Tyson leaned toward his partner and whispered something in his ear. She opened the
back door for them, and to her surprise, after
buckling Echo in, Tyson got in the back seat
as well.

"You guys okay back there?" Skylar asked.

Echo raised his head and woofed softly.
She chuckled. Tyson smiled almost apologetically.

"The vet assured me he's fine," Tyson said.

"Echo should be back on his feet tomorrow. I'm not supposed to push him but to let him set the pace. I'm probably just being a bit overprotective by sitting back here with him. But I'm worried he might get jostled."

"It's fine and don't apologize," she said. Her eyes met his in the rearview mirror. "It's kind of adorable actually and I'm sure he'd be even more protective of you if he thought you were hurt."

Tyson chuckled. "Ain't that the truth," he said. "I so much as trip on the carpet and Echo leaps to my side as if I can't be trusted to walk on my own."

She laughed too. "Well, I'll make sure I get both of you guys home safe."

"Sorry I took longer in there than I expected," he said. "Jodie had written up a proposal that she be allowed to take Shiloh home and train him as an American Sign Language hearing dog and I wanted to forward her email to SAC Bridges before I left for the day."

"That's wonderful," Skylar commented. "I hope it works out for her."

Tyson ran his hand over Echo's back. "Me too."

"That reminds me," she said. "Kate Montgomery asked me if I could meet her for brunch tomorrow. Apparently since she's been released from rehab she's been thinking about her next steps. Thankfully, I'm due for a morning off."

Tyson frowned. It had been six months since Kate had been found by the side of a road in Denver with no memory, her blazing car nearby—and an empty infant car seat and baby blanket on the ground. Baby Chloe Baker had been missing ever since, her mother found dead in her own car in a ditch. There were few leads, but the team was working hard on piecing together the puzzle.

Skylar assumed the fact the case was still unsolved weighed as heavily on Tyson's heart as it did hers. She'd felt close to Kate from the moment she'd seen her lying in a coma at the hospital, having been assigned as the liaison between the Denver PD and the RMKU, whose case it was. Kate was slowly recovering her memories and Skylar was hopeful that she'd make a breakthrough any day.

"Please give her my best," Tyson said.

"I will."

She drove through the city streets barely a mile above the speed limit. The sun was setting on the horizon, casting red and golden hues over the purple mountain ridges in the distance. She reached Tyson's house. To her surprise a small and very old looking Volkswagen sat in the driveway.

"You got a new car?" she asked.

He chuckled. "The elderly couple next door found out my SUV was in the shop and offered to lend it to me. They've probably left the key under the mat."

They left Echo in the car for a moment while they did a perimeter search of his house. There was no sign anything was amiss. Then, Tyson lifted Echo out of the vehicle and carried him to the house.

"Can you open the front door?" he asked.

"Absolutely," she said.

As she opened the door of Tyson's house, Echo barked quietly and wriggled in his arms, as if to announce he'd had enough of being carried and wanted to get back to being his regular independent self.

"All right, buddy," Tyson said. "Hold on."

He set the dog down gently. Echo limped through the front door, over to a dog bed on the far side of the room, and plopped down with a loud sigh.

"Come in," Tyson said. "Welcome to my home. I don't know if there's much space left on the coatrack, but you can put your stuff on the table."

Open concept with a living room area to her right and kitchen to her left, the house was cozy. In the living room, floor-to-ceiling bookshelves filled every available inch of wall space, many of which seemed to have extra books crammed in on top of those already on the shelf. The island separating the kitchen and living room was piled with even more books and gym equipment. She slid her gun, badge and cell phone into her bag and left them on the table. Then hung up her jacket on the coatrack and left her boots beneath it.

"I have these painkillers I'm supposed to mix into his food," Tyson said. "Which means I'm going to find something to bribe him with. Which should make him happy." He tossed his jacket onto the hook beside hers. "How would you feel about staying for dinner?" he added. "We could work on your warrant application to search Jason's trailer and I'd like to get a better handle on all this before my meeting with SAC Bridges tomorrow and I'd really appreciate it if you'd be able to spare some time to go over the case and see if we come up with any leads. I can't go too late, because I have to prepare for my meeting with SAC Bridges tomorrow. Plus, I don't know if I've got much of anything to cook. But if we can't rustle something up we can always order something in."

She felt a smile cross her face.

"I'd love that," she said. "Thank you. I'm sure we'll both think better when we're not working on an empty stomach."

She followed him into the kitchen. From her new vantage point she could now tell that along with a myriad of books, he also had a collection of records. While his house was more cluttered than she'd expected, it wasn't exactly messy. Everything had been stacked in neat piles or arranged in rows. He started pulling ingredients from his fridge and cupboard, one by one, and laid them along the counter.

"Okay, I've got ten eggs," he said, "one leftover hot dog, a little bit of ham but not enough for a full meal, two different types of cheese, some peppers, an onion, bread, olive oil, baking soda, a whole lot of spices and some crackers. Any thoughts?"

"How about a Denver omelet?" she suggested.

"I can't remember the last time I made an omelet without burning it and then trying to salvage it as scrambled eggs," he admitted. "I'm not much of a cook. I tend to put things on the stove, get distracted by something work related and burn it to a crisp."

"Well, fortunately for you I like cooking," she said. "It helps me think. There's something about it which I find so helpful and relaxing at the end of a long day. Plus, I don't do it as often as I'd like." Not to mention she could tell at a glance that his stove was a gas range with actual flames she could control the level of instead of a regular burner. "Why don't I cook us an omelet while you figure out how to trick Echo into taking his medicine?"

"Deal," he said. "But let me at least help you cut the veggies. I may not be much with a stove, but I'm great with a knife."

They stood side by side in his kitchen and divided up the ingredients. Tyson got out a frying pan. She found a clean bowl in the dish rack and a whisk hanging beside the stove. She drizzled the olive oil into the pan, and placed it onto a low burner to heat, then started cracking eggs into a bowl.

"I want to go back to Jason's trailer with a very strong and thorough warrant," she said. "If we can collect those bottles and cigarette butts and get them tested for DNA, that might lead us to who the kingpin is. But getting a warrant will mean making a case before my judge, but for now all we have is Bernie's testimony, some spray paint bottles and burned grass, and the fact Jason used to serve with the rangers. It's all very circumstantial."

Tyson frowned. "We need more."

He laid the mismatched pieces of ham he'd found in his fridge out on the cutting board and began chopping them into identical-sized squares.

"But the fact that we're being thorough and not cutting corners is better for us in the long run," he added, "because it means our case is much more likely to stick in court."

"True." She appreciated the fact Tyson thought that way too. She'd seen some cops get a bit reckless when going after a perp, only for mistakes they'd made or a lack of evidence to end up with the criminal being let right back on the street again. "As important as it is to get Jason Roque off the street, he's still just a small fish. Our ultimate goal is to catch the drug kingpin behind the operation."

"Agreed," Tyson said. "If we catch Jason and he doesn't flip on the kingpin, his boss will just send someone else after the RMKU."

"And Denver will still be flooded with illegal drugs," she said.

As she busied herself with making the dinner, Tyson cut the hot dog into pieces, dug little holes into the pieces and slipped the pills inside. Then he sealed the holes with peanut butter and offered them to Echo, who wolfed them down without so much as a sniff of complaint.

The pan was so wide she ended up making one huge omelet, stuffed thick with cheese and ham, which she cooked to a golden edge, and then cut in half for them to share.

They moved to the living room and sat on the couch.

"Looks amazing," Tyson said.

They talked through the case, slowly picking apart everything they knew and exploring it from every angle and brainstorming the next steps they could take. Usually she found herself worrying that her fellow officers might be impatient with how methodical she could be. But Tyson seemed genuinely interested in hearing what she thought and why. The conversation continued as they finished dinner, moved back to the kitchen and did the dishes together, before ending back up on the couch, this time sitting a little closer than before. Hours slipped by and Echo snored contentedly on his bed. Until she looked up and glanced at the clock to suddenly realize it was almost midnight.

Tyson saw it too. "Wow, I'm sorry. I had no idea," he said. "I completely lost track…"

"Me too."

He stood. So did she.

"I'm sorry to see you out, but I have a long day tomorrow," he said.

"Yeah, me too," she said. "Plus you've got your meeting with SAC Bridges."

But somehow they were both standing there and neither of them made a move toward the door, as if neither of them wanted to be the one to make the evening end. Finally, she stepped back, so did he and they started toward the door. She bent down and pulled her boots on. When she stood up, he was holding her jacket out for her.

"Here, let me help you," he said.

She turned around and let him help her into it. Her keys were in her pocket, but where had she left her bag? For a moment she couldn't remember.

Then she turned back to face him. An odd tension seemed to crackle in the air between them, as if the invisible strands that had kept them locked in conversation all evening were now sparking like severed power lines.

"Thank you for a wonderful night," she said.

"Thank you too," he said. "We should do this again sometime."

"We should," she said.

He slid his arms around her.

"Well, good night then," Tyson said.

They hugged.

"Good night," she said.

Then without stopping to think, she leaned forward, so did he and their lips met.

# TEN

They both leaped back at once, as if the furtive kiss had shocked them both and caught them by surprise. Skylar reached for the doorknob and repeated, "Good night," then she stepped out into the night. Her legs felt weak as she walked to her car, and she was surprised she didn't trip and fall. She opened her car door, climbed inside and then heard his front door close.

She sat there for a few seconds and pressed her cold hands against her flaming-hot cheeks.

Their lips had touched so lightly and for such a brief moment she'd barely felt the kiss. And yet the memory of it seemed to radiate through her as if she'd been sitting beside a warm fire. She'd just kissed Tyson, he'd kissed her, she had no idea which one of them had initiated the kiss and what's more she knew a large part of her would be very happy if it happened again.

Which it couldn't, she reminded herself firmly as she drove.

Neither of them had time for a relationship. He certainly didn't, considering everything on his plate. And she didn't want to let herself be emotionally compromised and thrown off course from the case she was working or the one which would come after it. Relationships were messy. People lost their sense of self in them. The drama of her parents' relationship had been all-consuming, ruining their lives and nearly destroying hers.

Even if she did have the time, which she didn't, it wasn't worth the risk.

Not even with a man as thoughtful, intelligent and caring as Tyson Wilkes.

It was a short drive home, barely five minutes, and she drove with the windows open, in the hopes the cold night air would knock some sense back into her racing heart. It wasn't until she'd parked in the driveway outside her small house and walked almost all the way to the door that she realized she'd left her bag with her phone, badge and gun inside it on the table at Tyson's house. She turned to go back.

The attacker came out of nowhere, grabbing her from behind and yanking her back. He was huge, tall and heavyset. Much larger than J-Rock. And she realized with a start he'd probably been waiting by her front door and if she hadn't turned around he'd have likely tried to grab her, force himself into her home with her and imprison her there. He shoved her hard against her car and pressed his weight against her back. One large hand clasped her shoulder. His fetid breath filled her nostrils.

Instinctively she reached for her weapon and then remembered she'd left it behind.

"Now, you're going to be quiet, stop fighting and let me in." The voice was male, deep and dripped with menace. "Once we're inside you're going to do exactly what I say and then you're going to call Tyson Wilkes for me. Otherwise, I'll make you suffer."

Faith, adrenaline and the determination to survive filled her core, fueling her mind to outsmart him and her body to fight him off. She was going to stay alive. She was going to defeat him.

"Who are you?" she asked, forcing her voice painfully through her throat. "What do you want?"

He didn't answer. She felt the sharp prick of a knife against her throat and knew he wouldn't hesitate to kill her. She kicked back hard, and felt his grip fall from her body as he grunted. He was still behind her, but now she had the space to turn to face him. She spun. Beady eyes glared at her through the holes in a ski mask. She didn't have enough room for a full-on punch but threw a sharp uppercut that caught him on the jaw. He swore and fell back. She pushed him hard with both hands and started to run toward the road. She could hear him chasing her. Where could she go? If she knocked on random doors he could catch up with her, force his way in and put more people in danger. There was a gas station a few blocks away, but would she make it there in time?

She screamed in fear and in fury, hoping someone would hear her and call 911. He threw himself at her in a tackle, catching her around the waist and knocking her forward. Her body hit the ground. His weight landed hard on her back.

"Now I'm going to make you pay," he snarled.

The sound of a tinny car horn filled the air, mingled with the furious sound of Echo barking. It was Tyson.

"This is your only warning," the attacker said. "Stop helping him. Stop talking to him. Or you'll be next."

Fear flooded Tyson's heart like a tidal wave threatening to overwhelm him when he watched through the small windshield of the Volkswagen as Skylar struggled bravely against the masked man crouching over her. He continued to lean on the horn hoping the noise of that and Echo's barking would give her the distraction she needed to escape. But he could barely hear the din over the sound of his own beating heart.

*Lord, help me reach her in time!*

Skylar rolled, tossing the man off her. She leaped to her feet. A knife glinted in his hands. Then he glanced at Tyson and they locked eyes, as if he was debating whether he had time to kill her in front of him right here and now. He was too big to be Jason. Was it the man he'd mistaken for Dominic? Tyson forced the small car faster. The man turned and ran toward an unmarked van, leaped in the driver's side and peeled off. Tyson swerved to a stop, yanked his seat belt off and threw the door open.

"Stay in the car," he ordered Echo, who barked in protest. "You're injured!"

The dog had been determined to come with him and considering the fact Echo was recovering from an injury and on painkillers, he hadn't wanted to leave the dog home alone.

Then he ran for Skylar and caught her and she stumbled into his arms. But as soon as he hugged her, she stepped back out of the embrace.

"Are you okay?" he asked.

Her clothes were muddy, but a bright fire filled her eyes as if a fire was alight inside her.

"I'm okay," she said and gasped a breath. "What are you doing here?"

"Two minutes after you left I realized you'd left your stuff on the kitchen table," he said. "I'm sorry I didn't notice sooner. But the moment I realized it I hopped in my neighbor's car and came over."

"He was waiting for me," she said, "hiding by my front door. I got out of the car, realized I'd left my bag behind at your house and immediately turned around to go back. If I hadn't he would've caught me by the door and might've forced me inside and—"

A sob choked the words from her throat before she could finish the sentence.

He took her face gently in his hands. He wanted to promise her that he'd keep her safe, protect her and make sure no one ever hurt her again. But he couldn't. Not now. He needed to think like a cop, figure out who this man was and how to stop him. But it was hard to think of anything with the sound of his own heartbeat pounding almost deafeningly in his ears.

"What did he want?" Tyson asked.

"He wanted me to go inside with him," she said. "But I wasn't about to let that happen. I think he was planning on hurting me and then calling you to lure you over."

He dropped his hands and stepped back. "He was using you as bait?"

She nodded. "Then when he realized he wasn't going to succeed in that, he told me that if I didn't stop helping you I'd be next."

She reached for his hands and grabbed them.

"He said *next*," she repeated. Her voice was urgent. "Which could mean he's already attacked someone else, maybe even killed them."

"If this is the kingpin," Tyson said, "then according to your contact Bernie he just got out of prison. Who else would he have gone after?"

Her eyes widened. "Do you think he could've gone after Jason Roque?"

"Maybe that's why we couldn't find him around his trailer or the campsite," he said.

"We'll take my car."

He nodded. "I'll drive," he said. "First, though, I'll just quickly text Nelson, Ben, Lucas and Gavin to alert them to what's going on, especially since they served with Jason and he might be in trouble. You call it in."

Within moments, Echo was buckled in Skylar's back seat, the text to his team had been sent and the three of them were heading to the Rockies.

Skylar finished the call and turned to him.

"I filed a police report and they've put out a BOLO for the man who attacked me," she said. "Denver PD are canvassing the area around my house. They're also sending backup to meet us at Jason's trailer. We should beat them there by a couple of minutes, but either way they've agreed to stay back in the woods and wait for my signal, because for all we know Jason is fast asleep in his bed right now, and we don't want to scare him into running."

The trees parted and this time he could see the badly painted pickup truck parked by the front door. A light was on inside the trailer and seeped out around the gaps in the cardboard. This time somebody was home. He pulled the car to a stop, unbuckled Echo's seat belt and again reminded the K-9 to stay in the car.

Echo whimpered impatiently, wanting to come with them.

"I'm sorry, buddy," he said, "tonight you're on lookout."

He pulled out his weapon and exited the car. So did Skylar. And that's when he realized someone had slashed all four tires on the truck.

Whoever had come to visit Jason's trailer hadn't wanted Jason to leave.

They drew closer and he realized the door was hanging off one of its hinges as if whoever had opened it had used such force they'd ripped it right off. Skylar raised her radio to her mouth and quietly called in what she was seeing, then put her radio down again.

"I'm going in," he said. "Stay back here and cover me."

He watched as she steeled a breath.

"I'll take the lead," she said, "and go in the

front door. You keep an eye on the outside in case somebody inside gets smart and tries to leap out a window."

Right. This was her case. She was the lead investigator, and he was there as K-9 backup.

"Sorry," he said. "I'm so used to taking charge I forgot this was your call. Sounds good."

She exhaled like she was relieved to hear him say that but he didn't know why.

"Thanks," she said. "If anyone tries to make a run for it, they'll run right into you."

"You got it," Tyson said.

He glanced at Echo. "And don't forget you're on lookout," he said. "If anyone tries to sneak up on us you let us know. Then once we get the all-clear I'll come and get you, and you can let me know if you find any drugs in the place."

Not that he had any doubt that they'd find some.

Echo sat up, his ears perked and he barked seriously.

"Is he actually trained as a lookout?" she asked.

"No," Tyson said. "But like I said before, Echo is a surprising dog and I've learned to never underestimate him."

They started toward the trailer. First Tyson

went wide and swept around the area, then he turned to her and said, "All clear."

She nudged the door open with her arm.

"Denver PD!" she called. "Identify yourself and come out with your hands up. We don't want any trouble. We just want to talk."

There was no answer. Nobody leaped out of the windows and made a bolt for it either.

She stepped through the door and then waved to Tyson to follow. He did so. The main room of the trailer was empty and had clearly been trashed. Every corner had been searched. Cushions had been ripped open and their stuffing yanked out in handfuls. Every cupboard was open and had been emptied. Empty bottles, some broken and some still intact, rolled toward them. Loose pills littered the floor.

He didn't see any weapons but his attention was drawn to a metal ammo can which lay on its side. He nudged it with his foot. Photos of men and women in military uniform spilled out and onto the floor.

Skylar waved him toward the closed door at the end of the trailer. He nodded. She started toward it while he watched the front door.

"Denver PD!" she called again. "We're not here to hurt you. I'm just opening the door."

She kicked the door and it flew open. He heard a small strangled sound leave her lips as if she'd barely managed to stop herself from screaming.

"Tyson," she called. "In here."

He walked to the end of the trailer. She stepped back and he looked through the doorway.

And saw Jason.

The former army ranger was lying on the bedroom floor. Blood spread out around him from what looked like a gunshot wound to his chest and another to his head.

Jason Roque was dead.

# ELEVEN

Emergency vehicles converged on the scene in minutes, casting the darkened night with the eerie blue, white and red tones of flashing lights. Tyson and Skylar secured the scene. Then Tyson stood back by the car with his hand on Echo's collar as the coroner took away Jason's body, forensic investigators in white protective gear pored over every inch of the trailer and campground, and Skylar coordinated the chaos.

He couldn't remember the last time he hadn't been the lead cop on a scene. Yet, he'd learned long ago on the battlefield that God had called him to be one part of a much larger whole.

Had he forgotten that in the past few months? Had he tried to do it all by himself?

He called Nelson, Ben, Gavin and Lucas, woke them up, filled them in and told them they'd meet first thing in the morning to talk further. The three that were local immediately offered to leap out of bed and drive out to assist. But he reminded them Denver PD had taken lead on the case and it was in the hands of the crime scene investigators now.

Then he'd told them to get some sleep; after all it was almost one in the morning.

He should probably hit the hay too. Not that he'd be able to get much shut-eye considering his meeting with SAC Bridges at noon. He'd hoped getting the extra twenty-four hours would give him the opportunity to catch whoever had been sabotaging the RMKU. They'd found Jason Roque, but now he was dead and they were no closer to figuring out who the kingpin was.

Somehow Tyson doubted that would be enough for SAC Bridges.

He closed his eyes and prayed.

*Help me, Lord. I need to save my unit. Identifying Jason was a big step forward. But now he's dead and catching the kingpin seems further away than ever.*

Maybe helping Skylar on her drug kingpin case had been God's way of reminding him that he shouldn't be trying to carry everything on his shoulders, but that he needed to be more open to accepting help and working as a team. He couldn't imagine where he'd have been without her or if he'd have taken the step to fill his team in as deeply as he had.

Skylar was an amazing cop. She had an incredible mind and there'd been something truly wonderful about cooking together, discussing the case for hours and just enjoying the company of this beautiful, incredible and talented woman, in a way he couldn't remember ever doing before.

He appreciated her more than she'd ever know. But he couldn't let an evening like tonight happen again. It wasn't just that he didn't have time for a relationship. He couldn't afford the distraction of one.

If he did somehow manage to talk SAC Bridges into giving him more time to address his concerns with the RMKU, he'd then be busy working every moment of every day to run the unit and prove that SAC Bridges's faith in him wasn't misplaced. And if the worst happened, and the SAC still felt the unit should close, Tyson would then be working just as hard to make sure every single person on his team, from the trainers to the officers, to Sydney, the veterinarian, and his assistant, Jodie, landed on their feet and ended up in the best possible place for them.

Either way, he didn't see a future with relaxing nights that were spent making inexpensive dinners out of the odds and ends he found in his fridge and where he was able to enjoy long and interesting conversations with a fascinating woman who made him feel happy and alive.

He looked up to see Skylar walking toward him. Emergency lights casting shifting shadows down her beautiful face and her strong form. She wasn't smiling, and somehow in that moment he realized he missed her smile more than he had words to say.

"I'm going to be stuck here until forensics are done," she said. "But the Denver PD officers are now returning to the city and they offered to give you a ride back."

"I appreciate that," he said. He'd come in Skylar's car and while he had absolutely no doubt that every single member of the RMKU would've happily driven out to pick him up, he also didn't want to be dragging any of them out of bed in the middle of the night when he could catch a ride back with another officer.

"And I appreciate your help on this," Skylar

said. And that's when he realized she wasn't meeting his eyes. Instead her gaze looked down at the ground by his feet. Somehow he missed her gaze even more than he'd missed her smile.

"When I first came to you for help with this I had no idea where this would lead," she said, "or how involved this would get. The good news is that I feel confident you'll be able to tell SAC Bridges that we've identified who committed the active acts of sabotage against you and the RMKU. It's still going to take some time to process everything we've collected. But even at this initial stage the evidence is pretty overwhelming. We've got the bomb-making equipment and fake blood, along with hand-drawn sketches of the RMKU building and handwritten notes planning the various attacks. His plans. Jason clearly did his homework for months to figure out all RMKU's vulnerabilities. Plus, there are a lot of notes on exactly what the drug boss he worked for wanted him to do. It's a slam dunk. I just wish he was still alive so we could find out *who* he was working for."

But would that be enough to convince SAC Bridges?

"I'm going to rack my brain on this," Tyson

said. "The answer to the kingpin's identity is somewhere in this mess, literally and figuratively. I'm missing something, and I don't like it."

Skylar nodded. "Whoever was giving him his marching orders was smart enough not to have his actual name or any identifying information on anything. We're still in the dark there. But there's still a lot more we have to analyze, including that ammo can filled with pictures. Hopefully there's an answer in there somewhere."

"Hopefully," he said.

He had to figure out the identity of the man who'd killed Jason and attacked Skylar tonight. Or why he had such a vendetta against Tyson. How long until this criminal found somebody else to do his dirty work? Would he go after Skylar again? Would he attack the other K-9 officers in the RMKU?

Would he finally come for Tyson himself?

"I know that the vendetta against me and the drug kingpin are linked," Tyson said. "But I'm still worried that working with me has put a target on your back."

At this, she finally met his eyes. But as he searched her face, it was like his usual ability to read her feelings in her eyes was gone completely, as if she'd somehow pulled heavy shutters down over his usual window inside her.

"My job puts me in danger," she said.

"I know, but this is something more than that—"

"Like I've told you before, I'm a cop," she said.

"I know, but—"

"That's who I am and I'm sorry if I've ever given you the impression otherwise," she said, her voice sharpening, "and if I have and that's why you tried to step in and take charge of securing the trailer."

What? No! How could she think that? He'd just momentarily forgotten she was the lead investigator on this case. Why was she reading so much into that?

"I know I messed up tonight," she went on. There was an edge that was almost bitter to her voice and he didn't know why. Was she angry at him? "I know what happened earlier tonight was unprofessional of me and that you have every right to report me to my superiors if you so choose—"

Hang on, unprofessional?

"What are you talking about?" he cut her off. "You've never been unprofessional around me. Not even for an instant."

Yes, they'd kissed. He still had no idea what he felt about that. In fact he'd decided that he didn't have the luxury of taking the time to figure it out. But they'd been off the clock and neither of them had done anything to feel ashamed of.

Skylar glanced over her shoulder as if to double-check nobody was nearby and in a position to overhear. Thankfully everyone was yards away and engrossed in their own work.

"I left my bag at your house," she said. "It had my phone inside, my badge and my gun..."

"Okay, I get why that's embarrassing," he said. "But you realized it almost right away and turned around to go back for it. Plus, it wasn't unsecured. It was at the house of a fellow officer who left to return it to you immediately." He knew plenty of officers who'd made much bigger mistakes and rolled with them as learning opportunities. He was sure she had too. "Why are you making such a big deal out of this?"

"Because when that guy attacked me, I had no weapon to defend myself with," she said, "I had no phone to call for backup and no badge to prove who I was if I managed to flag down help."

"Which I imagine was terrifying," he said. "But it was also a really terrible coincidence. Any other day, you'd have been reunited with your bag in five minutes and everything would have been fine. And yes, I know it could've been much worse. But thankfully I was there and had your back."

"I don't want to have to count on you being there," she said.

Something flashed in her eyes that was bright and unrelenting. And suddenly he understood how she felt. She was angry. Furious even. But she wasn't angry at him. She was angry at herself.

It was a feeling he knew all too well. He'd been angry at himself when the RMKU was sabotaged. He blamed himself for not catching Jason earlier. Even now he blamed himself for the fact he'd been killed before they'd reached him.

"I understand," he said.

"Then you can appreciate that while I'm incredibly thankful for everything that you and Echo have done to assist me on this case, I think it's time we wrap up this phase of the investigation," she said.

Hang on, why did it sound like she was saying goodbye?

"This is now a murder investigation on top of being a drug case," she said. "I know you've got a major parallel case into the same criminal from your own angle and that it will be important going forward that we compare notes and keep the lines of communication open. But I have to focus my attention on the fact we have a killer on the loose who may very well strike again. You have the K-9 unit to worry about with everything that entails. And while I am endlessly thankful for you and Echo, I think it's time for us to each run our own separate investigations." She ran her hands up over the back of her neck, scooped her hair up and tied it back into a bun. "To be blunt, I just can't see more nights like tonight, last night or the night before in my future."

Oh.

So, she was saying exactly what he'd been thinking. She was agreeing with him and even beating him to the punch. No more grabbing pizza, cooking together and poring over files late into the night. That meant logically speaking he should be agreeing with her, right? Maybe even be thankful that she'd been the one who'd said it first and that he could walk away from this whole situation without hurting her feelings.

Right?

So why did something inside him want very much to argue with her and tell her that she was wrong? Why did that part of him want to dig his heels in, tell her that she was worrying over nothing, because they were a strong team who made each other better not worse? Why did he want to suggest that, when all this was over, they should instead have more dinners, more conversations and more late-night walks getting pizza, when he knew far too well that he couldn't let that happen?

"You're absolutely right," he said, forcing himself to stick to his guns about what he'd been thinking before she walked up, and ignore whatever odd backpedaling his heart and mind were trying to do now. "I was just thinking the exact same thing actually and am relieved to hear you say it. I have to focus on my unit right now. Whatever comes next, I have to make the RMKU team my top priority and I can't afford any distractions."

She nodded. "Yeah, I get it."

"Besides," he said, "maybe if we stop spending time together Jason Roque's killer will stop seeing you as a target, which would be a good thing for your ability to conduct your investigation."

"You're right," she said, "when you put it that way. As much as I don't want to give anyone the impression I couldn't handle the pressure of having a killer on my tail, it definitely would make it harder to do my job and that's all that matters."

"For the record," he said, "I fully believe you can handle the pressure of absolutely anything you set your mind to."

She pressed her lips together and for a second he thought he saw the glimmer of a tear shine in the corner of her eye. Then she blinked hard and it was gone.

"Thank you," she said. "Look, for what it's worth, I really appreciate how much you've respected my role and thoughts in this case. I told you about my parents and how my father was controlling, mean to my mother and had to be right all the time. I think, on a subconscious level, part of me might've been worried that you might try to take over and undermine my authority. But you never did, not once, and I'm thankful for that."

He swallowed hard.

"Hey, maybe it was good for me to not be the boss for once," he said. "I liked working with you."

"I liked it too."

They both stood there a long moment looking at each other. He wondered if she felt the same pull to hug goodbye as he did. Finally, she stuck out her hand, he took it and they shook. When the handshake ended, she reached into her car, ran her hand over Echo's head and scratched the dog behind the ears.

"You're a very good dog, Echo," she said. "I hope one day I get to be partnered with a dog half as incredible as you." Then she turned to Tyson. "I'll send any more files or evidence that might be of interest to you to your office. I hope all goes well tomorrow. Well, I guess your meeting with SAC Bridges is actually today considering it's well after midnight."

"Thanks," he said. "I hope all goes well with your investigation."

"Good night. Tyson."

"Good night, Skylar. Take care of yourself."

"You too."

She turned and walked back toward the crime scene investigators without looking back. Not even two minutes later he was approached by a Denver police officer who offered to give him and Echo a ride home. He accepted the ride, gratefully, but asked to be dropped off at K-9 headquarters. Somehow he knew he wouldn't be able to sleep.

The K-9 unit was dark when he arrived and empty except for the night security officer doing his rounds. Tyson went into his office with Echo, where the dog promptly crawled into his crate and lay down inside it, with his head on its usual place on top of his paws resting just outside of the door. Tyson sat down at his desk and worked. He spent a couple hours on trying to figure out who the kingpin could be and coming up with nothing, the frustration helping to keep him awake. But the clock was ticking.

He shifted his attention to SAC Bridges's concerns about the unit again line by line. He wrote and rewrote his responses to each point. Eventually his body began to ache for sleep and his eyes grew so tired it hurt to blink. The clock on the wall told him it was almost four. Thankfully there was a cot in the break room, for officers who needed a rest after working overnight on a case. He brought its thin mattress into his office, set it on the floor beside Echo's cage and lay down. Just as he began to drift into sleep, he felt Echo curl up on the narrow mattress beside him.

He awoke just before nine, to the sounds

of people turning their computers on and the smell of fresh coffee brewing in the kitchen. He returned the mattress to the break room and took Echo outside for a gentle walk around the complex, happy to see that Echo was loping around at his usual happy pace, sometimes on three legs and others by gingerly using the leg which had stitches. Then Tyson splashed some water on his face, changed into a clean shirt, found some dog food for Echo and grabbed a muffin and coffee for himself and went back to work.

A few minutes later Jodie knocked on his doorframe and stuck her head around the corner. She had a smile on her face that was wide and infectious. And a white cardboard box in her hands.

"You know when I got in this morning I thought for once I'd actually beaten you in," she said, "until I spotted the two of you having a sleep over on the office floor. Everything okay?"

"Yeah, we just stayed up late preparing for the meeting today," he said. "What's up with you? You're practically beaming."

"SAC Bridges just called," she said. "He told me to tell you that he was looking forward to your meeting at noon. He also told me he'd approved my proposal to train Shiloh as an ASL hearing aid dog. I'm just so thrilled."

"So am I," he said and for the first time in hours he felt a smile spread across his face. "That's wonderful. I am so very happy for you."

Maybe as much as he hated the idea of the unit closing, if it did that would lead people into bigger and better things.

"How are you doing?" she asked.

He gave her a quick rundown of everything case related that had happened the night before, from the threat against Skylar's life, to finding Jason Roque dead in the trailer, to the evidence that led to them thinking they'd finally found the man who'd been sabotaging them, but only after it was too late to question him about who he was working for. Sadly they were no closer to figuring out who was ultimately behind the sabotage.

"Well, maybe this will help," Jodie said. She brought the box over to him. He took it from her and looked inside. It was the metal ammo container from the trailer, wrapped inside a large plastic evidence bag. "Skylar had this shipped over this morning from her precinct. She said she wasn't sure which officer would be the right one to assign to it but that she'd appreciate any assistance our unit could offer in figuring out who was in these pictures and what significance they might have to the case. They've already been dusted for prints, but the only ones found on them were those of the victim."

Huh. An odd and sad feeling settled in his stomach. So this really was it then. Skylar's days of calling him to talk about the case or dropping by his office were really over.

"Thank you," he said, "and congrats again about Shiloh."

She left with a smile. He found a pair of gloves and slid them on. Then he opened the plastic evidence bag and pulled out the ammo box. He lifted the heavy clasp and carefully spilled the pictures out onto his desk. Dozens of smiling faces of men and women in uniform looked up at him. They were all in black-and-white. He'd forgotten Jason had an interest in photography and had once wanted to be a photographer. Jason had actually had them developed and he wondered if Jason used to have his own darkroom. There were some familiar faces in the bunch and people he'd remembered serving alongside. Jason was in a lot of them himself, and Tyson presumed he'd used one of those small portable tripods. Memories of his time in the army rangers swept over him. The loose pills on the floor of Jason's trailer had been such a visceral and physical reminder of the fact Jason's life had gone off the rails since he'd left military service.

Tyson found himself praying. He thanked God for those he'd served with—those who'd gone on to live happy and fulfilling lives, those who were struggling, those who he served with now in the RMKU and those, like Jason, who'd lost their way.

His eyes glanced over the pictures, then one caught his eye.

It was Dominic Young.

The man who'd died on the battlefield helping him save Echo, and the soldier who'd been on his mind so often that Tyson for a moment had thought he'd seen him in Red Rocks Park the day before.

Carefully he nudged the picture free from the others and looked at it closer.

Dominic and Jason were standing side by side, in front of palm trees that looked far more like Beirut or Amman than anywhere in Afghanistan. While a generous smile beamed on Jason's face, the look in Dominic's eyes was more guarded and his tight smile was almost angry.

Skylar's words about everyone having secrets and nobody being perfect brushed his mind.

He was confused. When was this taken? He thought Dominic and Jason hadn't served together before that fateful mission when Dominic died. He looked closer. Along with the look in Dominic's eyes that wasn't quite right, there were tattoos on Dominic's arm that Tyson was positive he hadn't seen before.

He flipped the picture over and looked at the hand-printed date on the back. It had been taken almost a year after he and Gavin had carried Dominic's remains from the cave.

This wasn't Dominic. It couldn't be.

But then who was he?

# TWELVE

The Sixteenth Street Mall in downtown Denver was a pedestrian's paradise, filled with beautiful shops, fun eateries and absolutely no vehicles allowed except for the colorful hand-drawn rickshaws that ran up and down the cobblestones, filled with tourists who wanted an authentic slice of Denver life and romantic locals who were out on dates.

Skylar parked her vehicle in a large lot outside the area and walked down the busy sidewalk looking for the place Kate Montgomery had asked her to meet. It was the first time they'd see each other outside the rehab center Kate had been living in. She thought about all the time Kate had been in a coma, then her struggle to regain her memories, which were still sketchy. Someone had set Kate's car on fire and stolen the baby she'd been asked to care for—why, they didn't know—by little Chloe Baker's mother. That criminal was still out there. And so was Chloe. That Kate was out and about and talking about a surprise was a big deal.

As Skylar walked she thought about Tyson. According to a colleague in the Denver PD, Tyson had asked to be dropped off back at the RMKU building instead of his home. Skylar suspected that meant Tyson had spent all night there working. Part of her really appreciated his work ethic and dedication to his job. Another part of her knew how dangerous it could be not to have balance in life. Things like her weekly support group meeting helped keep her mind in focus. Meeting up with Kate regularly over the past few months had turned into one of the greatest joys and blessings in her life.

The small coffee shop turned out to be animal friendly, with a large sign saying pets were welcome. Her curiosity was definitely piqued. Now, why had Kate requested this particular place to meet? As she stepped inside the door, she saw the woman sitting at a small table by the window. Petite and slight, with a curly brown bob, green eyes and a kind heart that never ceased to surprise Skylar with its capacity to care for others, over the past few months Kate had become far more than a victim in a case Skylar was working. She'd become a dear friend.

Kate waved cheerfully. A small dog with a goofy grin and a shaggy coat the color of chocolate brownies sat on Kate's lap, sporting a colorful collar.

"Who's this?" Skylar asked, delighted.

"Meet Cocoa," Kate said. "He's my emotional support therapy dog."

"He's lovely," Skylar said. She reached out her hand for Cocoa to sniff.

The dog licked her hand and Skylar petted his head.

Then Kate reached up and gave Skylar a hug. "I know at some point I'll have to teach him that he can't always sit on my lap. But I like having him close. Especially when we're sitting on the couch and he cuddles up next to me. Having him sleeping there beside me is really good for nightmares too."

Skylar sat in a seat across from Kate. A waitress materialized by their side. Both women ordered coffee and said they needed a moment to look at the menu.

"I've been feeling nervous about what my next step would be after I left rehab," Kate said. "I've been hoping my memory would've

fully returned by now. But it's still so patchy."
She frowned. "I wish I could remember what
I was doing in that car with a baby. I do
vaguely remember knowing Chloe's mother,
Nikki, but not why she entrusted me with
Chloe. Who set my car on fire? Who killed
Nikki and tried to kill me? Who kidnapped
Chloe? And why?" She shook her head, her
green eyes troubled. She looked down at the
sweet dog on her lap, and Skylar could see
the comfort that Cocoa brought Kate.

Skylar reached across the table and squeezed
her friend's hand.

"I wish I could give you those answers and
assurance that all your memories will come
back," Skylar said. "But I do know that no
matter what happens I have faith that God
can bring wonderful things into your life and
that I'll be here for you, whatever you need."

"Thank you," Kate said. Tears glimmered
in her beautiful eyes. "I do have an idea about
what my next step should be."

"Really?" Skylar said and sat back.

"I feel like I should go back to Montana,"
she said. "I've been looking at a map and
there's an area I feel so drawn to called Sercy.
I have no idea why, though. I wonder if I'll
find the answers I'm looking for. I just know

I want to live in a cabin, somewhere close to there. And I see myself looking out at the vista, sketching in a drawing pad. Almost like sketching will reveal something I've forgotten."

"Maybe it will," Skylar said with a nod. "And I can help you find the perfect place. Beautiful and remote but close enough to civilization that if you need help, you'll have it."

Kate nodded. "Going to Montana feels right."

"Well, I'm going to miss seeing you so often," Skylar said.

"I'm going to miss you too," Kate said.

"I'll work with you to find you and Cocoa a really wonderful place," Skylar said, "and provide you all the help you need as you settle in."

"Thank you," Kate said.

The waiters arrived with a metal carafe of coffee, two mugs and a plethora of sugar and cream.

They sat in relaxed quiet for a long moment, sipping their coffee. Then Kate asked, "So how are you doing?"

Skylar filled her in a bit about her week, without mentioning any of the details of the case she'd been working on, that she'd partnered with the RMKU or even that the "officer" she'd been working with was Tyson. Something about telling the story that way made Skylar find herself opening up to her friend about the emotional moments of the week, how she'd felt and what she'd experienced inside. It was like the difference between describing a journey by listing off stops on a map as opposed to the surprise of seeing a brightly colored mailbox or the joy of watching a waterfall flow under a bridge you crossed.

She found herself admitting how much she'd enjoyed working with the unnamed officer, the thrill of finding evidence and the happiness of working together over dinner with him.

She even admitted the kiss.

"Sounds like you really have some feelings for this guy," Kate said, gently.

Did she have feelings for him?

"No, I don't," Skylar said. It had been a knee-jerk reaction and Kate's raised eyebrows showed her that her friend didn't believe it for a second. "I mean, yes, I do. But not clear-cut 'feelings.'" She moved her fingers in air quotes. "It's more like a complicated mess of too many emotions at once."

"I'm not in a place to give you advice," Kate said, "especially as I remember so little of my life before you and I met. But you're an absolutely amazing person and I trust you with my life. So, I think you should trust your heart on this."

"My mother lost herself when she fell in love with my father," Skylar admitted, "and she's not the first person I've met who lost themselves in a relationship."

"I know," Kate said, "but you're not her."

The conversation turned back to Kate's art therapy, her hopes for Montana and the potential it could unlock more memories.

Was this going to be the answer to helping them finally solve what had happened to her and find baby Chloe? Skylar hoped so.

After a long and happy brunch, it was time for Skylar to get back to work. She gave Kate a long hug and Cocoa another pat and then started back to her car.

Her phone buzzed. She looked down and felt her eyes widen. It was a text from Bernie.

Officer Morgan! I need help! I was hanging with some friends and they got really mad I told you about J-Rock.

She sighed. Yeah, Bernie had taken quite a risk telling her everything he had. Before she could reply her phone buzzed again.

They drove me to Fault Cave and left me. I got no way to get home. I'm scared. What if they come back and do something to me?

She texted him back quickly.

It's going to be okay. Just tell me where you are and I'll come get you.

Seconds passed without a reply. Then he sent her his GPS location.

Hurry! My phone is gonna die.

Her footsteps quickened.

I'm on my way.

He didn't reply. She called Bernie once she was alone in her car, but it went straight to voice mail. His phone must have died. She debated calling Tyson, giving him an update on Bernie and asking if he'd managed to find anything interesting in the photos. But his meeting with SAC Bridges was in a little over two and a half hours, and she reminded herself that he was busy. Plus, the sooner she got used to not wanting to talk to him about every little thing in her case the better.

Fault Cave consisted of a whole network of claustrophobic tunnels just east of the town of Golden. The fact that it was off the beaten path and easy to get lost in meant it avoided getting the crush of tourists that Red Rocks Park did, and tended to draw only the most ambitious and adventurous spelunkers. The parking lot was empty when she pulled in, except for the miserable-looking figure of Bernie sitting alone under a tree. She parked the car and walked over to him.

"Hey," she called. "Sorry you got stranded. Ready to go back to town?"

The teenager looked down at his shoes and didn't meet her eyes.

"Listen," she said. "I'm not angry at you for dropping off the grid like that and I'm not here to judge you. I'm just here to help."

Bernie looked up. Panic filled his eyes as if his mind was in turmoil. Then suddenly he shouted, "Run! It's a trap! I'm sorry. He threatened to kill my girlfriend if I didn't give him my phone to lure you out here!"

She hesitated for a moment and then reached for her weapon.

"Come on," she said. "Just get in the car and you can tell me everything as I drive. I'm not leaving you here!"

But it was too late. Suddenly she was grabbed from behind. The horrible smell from the night before filled her senses along with the menacing voice that sounded like the thing of nightmares.

"You got nowhere to run." He pressed a sickly sweet rag over her face so tightly she could barely breathe. "This time you're not getting away from me."

# THIRTEEN

Tyson stood in his office, leaning against his desk in the same place he'd been when he talked to Nelson, Ben and Gavin yesterday morning. This time Gavin was on his right, Ben in the middle and Nelson to his left, as if the three men had silently decided to play musical chairs. Shadow, Koda, Diesel and Echo lounged in various spots around the room.

This time he had Lucas and Angel too, joining him on his laptop by video call. His black-and-white border collie was beside him. He set the laptop on the side of his desk and turned the screen so that the men could all see each other.

Then he glanced at the clock. It was eleven fifteen. It had taken more time to get everyone here than he'd hoped. SAC Bridges would be there in forty-five minutes, but the question on his mind was too important to wait.

Silence fell over the men as he passed around the photo that had been found in the trailer.

"What do we know?" Tyson asked. "Right now, I need actual facts. Not guesswork."

"We lost our friend Dominic Young in battle," Gavin said. There was a solemnity to his voice that reminded him of the moment they'd bowed their heads at Dominic's graveside. "That's an irrefutable fact."

"Agreed," Tyson said. "So say we all."

The men murmured and nodded.

"So, clearly whoever the man in this picture with Jason Roque is, it's not Dominic," Ben said. "Looks a lot like him, though. Also a fact. Enough alike to be his brother."

"Dominic told me he was an only child," Gavin said.

"He told me that too," Ben said.

"Me too," Lucas agreed.

Once again Skylar's words filled his mind. *In the real world nobody is actually perfect. We've all made mistakes or missteps.*

"Dominic told me that too," Tyson said. "But he might not have been telling the truth. I thought I saw him yesterday. Just for a moment, and I can't be sure what I saw, but I thought it was him."

Gavin cleared his throat.

"I was sure I saw Dominic watching us from a distance when we were at his graveside," Gavin said. "I thought I was seeing things so didn't tell anyone."

"So, logically we're thinking Dominic has a brother who looks a lot like him. Maybe even a twin he never told us about?" Nelson said.

"If so, it's a twin he actively lied about," Lucas said.

Tyson blew out a hard breath.

"Dominic lost his parents when he was a teenager," he said. "He had very high standards for himself and others. Maybe they had a falling-out and became estranged."

"That gets into the realm of guesswork," Nelson said. He leaned back in his chair and crossed his arms. "But it's not a bad guess." Then suddenly he sat up straight. "I just remembered something! This little old lady, I think she was a great-aunt of Dominic's, came up to me after the funeral and asked me if I knew Daniel. I thought she meant Dominic and was just confused."

Jodie's head appeared in the doorway.

"Everything okay?" she asked. "I thought I heard somebody shout."

"Yeah, that was Nelson," Tyson said. "We just collectively figured out that our friend

Dominic Young, who died in Afghanistan, might've had an estranged brother named Daniel, and that he might be who we're looking for."

"Your meeting with SAC Bridges is in less than forty minutes," she said.

"I know," Tyson said. "But this is urgent. This guy could be the drug kingpin Skylar is after and the thug who's been sabotaging our unit and targeting both me and Skylar. Not to mention a killer. The sooner we find his name, both Skylar and I can go after him. She can crack her case and I can save the unit."

Jodie disappeared back through the doorway and returned immediately. "How can I help?"

"Check crime records and news stories for a Daniel Young," Tyson said. He glanced at Lucas on his screen. "You too." He reached for the box of files Skylar had brought over that in the chaos of the past couple of days they still hadn't gone through. "Everybody else, dig in."

They passed the files around and started reading, flipping through them with urgency. Several tense minutes ticked by.

"Got it!" Ben called and leaped to his feet. "Daniel Young convicted of aggravated assault and drug charges."

He held up the file toward them. Tyson leaned forward as did the others.

Daniel's mug shot looked a whole lot like Dominic.

"I've got an attempted murder charge!" Gavin yelled.

"And I've found an old high school graduation announcement," Jodie said. Her fingers moved quickly. "No photos, but it lists both Dominic and Daniel Young as graduating students."

"And I've found another murder charge," Lucas said.

Tyson ran his hand over the back of his head. Had they finally found the person behind all this?

"Also, you're down to fifteen minutes," Jodie said. "And SAC Bridges is never late."

Tyson glanced to the clock. They were out of time.

"Okay, let's leave it here for now," he said. "I'm going to give Skylar a quick call and fill her in on what we've got." He dialed her phone and waited while it rang. Then it clicked. Silence fell on the other end. Had he gotten her voice mail?

"Hi, Skylar," he started, "it's Tyson—"

"Hello, Tyson," a male voice responded. "I was wondering when you'd call."

Tyson felt his face pale. Quickly he signaled the others to listen and put the phone on speaker.

"Who is this?" he asked. "Where's Skylar?"

"Safe for now," the voice said. It was deep and rang with malice, and Tyson realized that although Skylar had described the voice of the man who attacked her, he'd never actually heard it. If he had, would he have recognized it? He didn't know, but he did now. It was like a distorted, warped version of Dominic's. "I'm sending you her GPS coordinates now. Meet me there. Come alone. If I see so much as a second vehicle, a shadow or a chopper in the sky, I will hurt her."

The phone went dead. Tyson's blood ran cold. He glanced around the room at the ashen faces around him.

"I'm going with you," Gavin said. "You're not doing this alone."

"You can't let him see you." Ben turned to Gavin. "We need Daniel to think Tyson's come alone. I suggest he drive your SUV and you hide in the back with Koda. Also we'll coordinate a wider rescue effort on the perimeter."

"Don't worry about your meeting with SAC Bridges," Jodie told Tyson. "I'll explain you had an emergency and that you've gone after the mastermind behind both the drug case and the sabotage."

"I think I'll go ask Bridges if I can talk to him about his concerns," Nelson said. "If that's all right with you, boss. I get you've been handling it, but maybe the perspective of somebody in the trenches will help."

"I will too," Ben said.

"You can count me in," Lucas said. "After all, I'm out in the field right now and have been coordinating with Chris back at headquarters. That might add some perspective."

"Sure." Tyson nodded and realized he felt too numb to even fully process what was happening. He gestured to the yellow pads on his desk. "My notes are right there. Help yourself."

"Good to go?" Gavin asked.

Tyson felt the weight of the room on his face. Their backs straightened as if standing at attention. Waiting for their marching orders. He glanced down at his partner. Echo looked up at him with more trust than Tyson knew how to absorb. And he realized for the first time he didn't know what to say.

"I can't bear the thought of anything happening to her," he admitted to his colleagues, "and I'm worried it'll throw me off."

Nelson and Ben shared knowing glances.

"You're not alone," Jodie said, firmly. "We've got your back. Now go."

Tyson signaled to Echo and they ran from the room, with Gavin and Koda on their heels.

His chest hurt so much he had to gasp for every breath.

He had to reach Skylar. He had to save her.

The thought of losing her made him more scared than he'd ever been in his life.

The first thing that Skylar became aware of as her aching body swam back into consciousness was the heavy weight of something pressing against her front, back and shoulders, like her body armor vest, only much bulkier and heavier. She was wedged sitting upward at an odd angle, propped against something uncomfortable she couldn't see. Her hands were tied behind her back. Darkness filled her eyes and thick fabric gagged her mouth, making it harder to breathe. She forced herself to take a deep breath in through her nose to center herself and calm her nerves and smelled the scent of damp earth and gasoline.

Fear sent hot tears rushing to her eyes. She closed her lids and prayed for help.

"Skylar!" Tyson's voice filtered at the edges of her consciousness.

Her eyes shot open. Was he really here? Had he found her?

Then she heard the sound of Echo barking. The dog's strong and determined woofs echoed in the darkness.

*I'm here! Tyson, I'm here!* She tried to scream but the gag was so tight she barely made more than muffled sounds. Hope rose in her chest as she heard Tyson and Echo come closer. Then she saw the flicker of a flashlight dancing in the darkness ahead down what she could now see was a narrow tunnel. The light grew brighter, illuminating the doorway of the tunnel ahead of her. Then Tyson burst through a doorway to the cave with Echo, leashed and harnessed by his side.

"Skylar!" As Tyson's eyes met hers, her name escaped his lips in a deep and gravelly rasp. As if the depths of emotion inside him had overwhelmed his ability to speak. "Are you okay?"

She nodded. Wishing she could call out to him. The beam of his flashlight swung over the cave, illuminating the scene around her.

The cave was as large as a living room. Red jerricans of gasoline were stacked two deep along one wall of the room with what looked like white blocks of plastic explosives duct-taped to them.

She looked down at her chest. She was wearing an explosives vest. The man who'd kidnapped her had rigged her to explode.

"Don't worry," Tyson said, "we're going to call for the bomb squad and get you out of here."

He stepped toward her. Too late she saw the thin wire stretching out across the ground in front of her.

*Tyson!* she tried to yell through her gag. *Stop!*

But it was too late—within a second he'd tripped the wire.

Her vest beeped. Bright red and flashing numbers radiated from her chest.

Tyson dropped to his knees in front of her.

"I'm so sorry," he said as he gently, carefully, pulled the gag from her mouth. Tenderly he brushed his hand along her jaw. He was so close now she could feel his breath on her face. But he pulled back and hovered just inches away as if he was afraid to touch her.

"Whatever you do, don't take the vest off,"

she said. "I'm sure it's rigged to explode if you tamper with it."

He nodded. Anguish filled his eyes.

"How long have we got?" she asked.

"Five minutes," he said. He grabbed his phone and his radio. But the phone had no signal and the radio buzzed with static. "I can't reach anyone. We're in here pretty deep. Gavin and Koda are hidden nearby, but even if I run out there and call for them, they won't get here in time."

She leaned toward him. Her forehead brushed against his.

"I want you to run and save yourself," she said. "I don't want you to die here with me."

"I know," he said. "Because that's exactly what I'd say to you." She heard his voice catch in his throat. "But you know I'm not going anywhere without you."

She did. She didn't know how she knew it. Only that here on the brink of danger, that same invisible thread which she'd felt between them in his living room was still holding them tight.

Echo whined softly as if wishing he could help.

"You know my dream is to work in explosives detection," she said. "I've done a lot of research into how bombs are made—and how to disarm them. If only I could see it, I might be able to defuse it. Or at the very least disconnect my vest from the timer and jerricans around me. We know Jason was an amateur. If this is one of his bombs it shouldn't be too complex."

"Then let me be your hands and eyes," Tyson said. "I'll explain what I'm seeing and you tell me what to do."

"Okay." She closed her eyes and tried to calm her breathing. "Focus on the explosive," she said. "What do you see? Describe it in detail."

For a moment silence fell, then she heard Tyson's voice in her ear, calm, confident and steady, helping her draw a mental picture of the bomb.

"I think I've got it," she said. "But what if I'm wrong? We could die in here."

"Listen," Tyson said. "I trust you with my life."

"And I trust you."

She started to give him instructions, haltingly at first, then growing in confidence as she told him which wires he could safely cut and which to wiggle. He was patient and gentle with her, as if he could sense how terrified she was and that didn't sway him one iota about placing his life in her hands.

Then she heard the sound of something click in the darkness from the corner of the cave. Her eyes shot open as fear coursed through her core, expecting a detonation. But instead a distorted voice filled the cave around them to boom and echo all directions at once.

"Just two rules," her attacker's voice taunted. "Run before the boom and nobody dies today. Nobody dies today. Everybody dies today." The voice laughed. It was an ugly and vicious sound. "Just two rules…"

The voice repeated the message from the start.

But she felt Tyson touch the sides of her face and pull her attention back to him.

"It's just a recording," Tyson said. "Is that the voice of the man who did this to you?" he asked.

"Yeah," she said.

"His name is Daniel Young," he said. "He's Dominic's brother. You were right—Dominic had a secret he was hiding from us. There was a picture of Daniel and Jason in the ammo container you had delivered to me this morning and we figured it out."

"Nobody dies today," the voice repeated in a taunting way. "Everybody dies today."

"This was probably something he rigged up to hit when the counter hit a certain moment," Tyson said. "Block him out. He doesn't matter. All that matters is you and me, and you telling me what to do next."

She felt something warm against her leg and looked down to realize Echo had curled up beside her protectively. She took a deep breath. "Okay."

They went back to the explosive device, with her focusing on Tyson, listening to his words and guiding him through the next step, as if nothing else mattered. Suddenly, a long and sharp beep sounded from her vest like a metallic scream. Tyson pulled her to him and cradled her against his chest. She closed her eyes.

*Lord have mercy on us.*

If this was the moment their lives ended, Tyson had chosen to be there with her, and she'd chosen to trust him.

The beeping stopped. So did the taunting voice.

She looked up at his face. "What happened?"

He sat back.

"The timer has gone dead," he said, with a noise that sounded like a cross between a laugh and a sob choking his voice. "You did it."

"We did it," she said. "But I've still got this

vest on and the slightest bump or impact could still make it blow. I need you to help me to my feet, very carefully. And then we walk nice and slowly back to the road to call Gavin for help."

"Deal," he said.

Carefully, he took her by the elbows and helped her up to standing. Then he moved behind her and cut her hands free. Gingerly he brought them around in front of her and massaged feeling back into her fingers.

"I really want to hug you," she said. "But I'm literally explosive."

He chuckled.

"But not for long," he said, and his words filled her with hope.

Tyson leaned toward her, and he brushed the faintest of kisses on her lips. Then he straightened back up again.

"We're going to get out of here, and we're going to get help," he said.

Slowly they started walking toward the entrance of the cave.

Footsteps sounded down the tunnels toward them. Someone was coming.

"Step behind me," Tyson said, softly, "please."

Echo growled. She stepped behind Tyson, and he pulled his weapon.

A man appeared through the doorway. He

was clutching a handgun. This time he was unmasked, and she recognized him as the man who'd been standing with Jason Roque in one of the military pictures she'd sent Tyson. For a moment he looked confused, and she suspected he was wondering why his bomb hadn't gone off. Then he locked eyes with Tyson and venom filled his face.

"Daniel Young," Tyson said. "You're under arrest for the murder of Jason Roque, and the attempted murder and kidnapping of Denver PD Officer Skylar Morgan. For starters. You have the right to remain silent. Anything you say can and will be used against you in a court of law."

Daniel turned and pointed the gun at them.

"I don't know how you did this to my bomb," Daniel said. "But it doesn't matter. I know how this is going to end. One way or the other. I'm going to kill Skylar and Echo and there's nothing you can do to stop me. Now you can either die along with them like you deserve. Or you can run like a coward and leave them to die just like you did to my brother."

# FOURTEEN

Tyson felt his heels dig hard into the cave's stone floor as he turned and faced the man who'd been tormenting him, hurting his dogs, threatening Skylar and trying to destroy the Rocky Mountain K-9 Unit for the past six months.

"Now put your gun down," Daniel said. "Or I'll shoot you both where you stand. I only need to get one good shot in Skylar's vest, and the whole cave will blow."

In any other circumstances Tyson might've risked a firefight, even though they were in a cave, counting on his ability to outmatch Daniel. But he couldn't risk a hit. Not here in this tight space, filled with accelerant and Skylar rigged to blow.

He put his gun back in his holster and raised his arms.

Firepower wasn't going to end this one.

This time he'd have to talk his way out of it. He just prayed and hoped his words could make a difference.

"I'm not going to run," Tyson said. "I don't know how long you've been planning this sick little game, who you've convinced yourself I am or what kind of ending you imagined this having. But it ends here and now. You're going to let Skylar and Echo walk out of here. Nobody else is going to die today."

Daniel snickered. It was an ugly sound.

"My brother died because of you!" His voice rose. "Jason told me you looked them all right in the eye and told them 'Nobody is going to die today,' and then you and the others just ran out of those caves and left him there to die!"

"I don't know what Jason told you," Tyson said. Or why. Or how Daniel had then twisted it in his mind. "But your brother's death was a tragedy."

Unexpected emotion pushed through his voice as he remembered the way the five of them had met in the office reminiscing about Dominic earlier that morning.

"To be honest, I never got over it," Tyson said. "And I know other members of my unit feel the same way. He was a good man and a great army ranger. He volunteered for a dangerous mission. He knew the risks. And we were destroyed when he didn't make it back alive."

"You let him die!" Daniel shouted, as if he needed to cling to the words to keep other troubling thoughts at bay. "You don't deserve to live!"

Motion drew Tyson's attention to the right. And that's when he realized that Skylar had silently stepped out from behind his protective shield and was slowly making her way around the right side of the cave.

"Don't move!" Daniel shouted, suddenly noticing it too.

Tyson realized what she was doing. She was drawing Daniel's attention away from him and making him focus on two different directions. As long as he and Skylar weren't together, Daniel wouldn't be able to shoot them both in rapid succession. And once he fired at one of them, the other would be able to jump on him and surprise him.

It was a brilliant plan, Tyson thought, except for the small hiccup that one of them was literally at risk of detonation.

"Don't look at her, look at me," Tyson yelled. "I'm the one you're angry at. She never even met Dominic. I'm the one you blame for your brother's death."

That did it. Daniel swung the barrel of his gun back at Tyson.

"That's right!" Daniel shouted. "I didn't even know how he died or what had happened until I had to bribe Jason with pills to tell me. Lousy junkie. I didn't even feel welcome at my own brother's funeral because we'd been estranged for years."

"And I'm sure that hurt," Tyson said honestly, feeling another pang of sympathy for the man standing there threatening to kill him. Daniel had said he wanted revenge. He acted as if this whole thing was about vengeance against the man who he'd thought was responsible for his brother's death. But what if it was about something more? What if deep down Daniel was jealous or resentful of the army rangers who'd embraced Dominic as a brother and been close to him before he died?

What if he hadn't been able to face his own hurt, shame and regret, and so it metastasized into something evil?

"I'm sorry he died before you reconciled," Tyson said. "And I'm sorry the rest of us didn't know about you sooner. Maybe if I'd been able to talk to him about you, it might've helped. I honestly don't know. But I would've tried and made sure you were invited to the funeral."

He watched out of the corner of his eye as Skylar slowly moved farther around the side of the room, growing closer and closer toward the door.

"If it wasn't for you and that dog my brother would be alive," Daniel shouted. "All of you, every single member of his unit, did nothing to help Dominic. And then you all get to come back here and set up your own little police force, right in my own backyard where you can all play cops and robbers and pretend to be heroes. You show up here and come after my guys and try to shut down my business like you're somehow better than me? When you all have blood on your hands?"

Tyson felt the hackles rise on the back of his neck. He couldn't take much more of this. Yes, he was buying time for Skylar to get into position and be able to escape so that she could get to Gavin and Koda. But he couldn't just stay there and let Daniel talk about his team this way. He wanted to yell back. He wanted to tell Daniel that a low-level criminal and killer like him didn't have the right to talk about the brave men, women and K-9s he served with.

Instead Tyson gritted his teeth and tried to imagine what Skylar would say in the face of an ugly outburst like this. She had depths of compassion that he'd never tapped in himself, but that he wanted for his own life. She sought justice that was flooded in mercy.

*Lord, help me do the same. Help me find the right words to say. For all our sakes.*

"I can't undo what's been done," Tyson said. "There have to be consequences to the things that have happened. But I promise I'll do what I can to make sure you also get the help you need. And once all this is over, I will visit you and talk about your brother."

He stretched out a hand in the open space between them, toward the man who'd spent the past few months trying to destroy everything Tyson cared about.

"I forgive you," Tyson said. He could still do everything in his power to arrest Daniel, bring him to justice, dismantle his operation and make sure he spent the rest of his life behind bars. But with God's help, he was willing to find the ability to forgive him. "And I'm sorry for not doing more to make sure your brother made it out of those caves alive. We got separated in there and I didn't find him again until it was too late. Please forgive me."

For a long moment, Daniel just stood there and didn't respond. Tension crackled in the air, as if all of his anger and pain was enough to detonate the explosives surrounding them and envelop them all in fire.

Then Daniel swore.

"I don't want forgiveness," he said. "I want revenge."

He turned and fired toward Skylar. But she was already gone and through into the entrance of the tunnel. The bullet ricocheted off the empty cave wall where she'd been just moments before. Tyson threw himself at Daniel and knocked him to the ground. The gun flew from his hands. Daniel swung back hard and caught Tyson in the jaw. Then the bigger man jumped on him in a flurry of blows.

But all that mattered now was making sure he stopped Daniel from getting that gun. They'd already survived one gunshot going off in the cave.

He knew they wouldn't survive a second.

"Skylar!" Tyson shouted. "Keep running! Don't stop!"

Skylar froze as she heard the sound of the gunshot echoing toward her and Tyson's faint voice telling her to keep running. Then she pushed herself to keep moving. Despite wanting to go back and see if he was okay, if she could help, she did as he asked, racing blindly down the long dark tunnel, feeling her way along the walls and trying to keep from tripping and falling. The weight of the explosive vest pressed against her, making it harder to breathe. The sound of Tyson and Daniel fighting for the gun echoed from somewhere deep inside the caves behind her.

She prayed with every step that Tyson would disarm Daniel, that he and Echo would make it out safe and this all would end peacefully.

*And thank You, Lord, for sending him to save me.*

She stubbed her toe on a rock, stumbled and nearly crashed headlong into a wall. Her palms smacked against the stone and she barely stopped the vest from smashing into it. Her heart pounded so hard inside her rib cage she feared that it would be enough to set it off.

She forced herself to keep running. Then the air grew lighter. Sunlight was filtering through the tunnel ahead of her. A few more steps and she could see the opening of the cave itself. She pushed through and blinked as sunlight filled her eyes.

She looked around and found herself in a remote section of Fault Cave away from the main entrance. There was a road down the hill to her right. She ran for it, jogging as fast as she dared, and remembered what Tyson had said about Gavin and Koda hiding nearby.

"Gavin!" she shouted. "Gavin, it's Skylar! You have to call backup! Tyson is in the cave with Daniel Young, and he has the whole room filled with gasoline and plastic explosives."

In an instant, she saw Gavin and his K-9 partner running toward her up the hill. Gavin was shouting into his radio for backup. Koda barked a warning sound that sent chills through her core and Gavin froze in his tracks. His partner sensed the bomb.

"Stay back!" she shouted. "I'm wired with explosives. There was a timer and we managed to disarm it. But the vest itself is still live."

She watched as Gavin blew out a long breath.

"Okay," he said. "Stand still. I'm going to come to you and let me see if I can get this thing off you. Looks like you've already done a lot of the work for me. I just need to finish the job." His Adam's apple bobbed. "Thankfully, emergency services and a whole lot of backup are on their way."

She prayed for Gavin as he approached her slowly and then gingerly unwound and dislodged wire after wire from the vest. Her eyes searched the mouth of the cave above her, hoping to see Tyson and Echo run through.

Hoping Tyson was still alive.

She needed to see his face again. She needed to wrap her arms around him and tell him how she felt about him sooner.

Emergency sirens filled the air. Help was on the way. Gavin let out a hard breath.

"Okay, I think we're good," Gavin said. "I'm just going to help you out of it now."

He took hold of the explosives vest and lifted it off her. Relief filled her core.

"Thank you," she said.

"No problem," Gavin said. "To be honest you'd already done most of the work. I just did the finishing touches."

Thanks to Tyson. She thought about those moments in the cave, being one breath away from death, with her life in his hands, and his life in hers. She'd never doubted, not even for a moment, that she'd been safe with him. A cavalcade of emergency vehicles, including paramedics and police, was coming down the road toward them.

She turned to Gavin. He was holding the explosives vest away from himself as if it was a smelly fish he wasn't sure where to drop.

"You coordinate law enforcement," he said. "I'll dispose of this safely, then I'll go inside the cave to disarm the explosives and help Tyson."

But even as they said the words, she heard the sound of another gunshot reverberating from somewhere deep inside the tunnel, followed by the sound of an explosion ripping through the rock and rumbling toward them.

Her heart stopped. No! It was too late. The tunnels were caving in on themselves. And Tyson and Echo were trapped somewhere inside.

She had to save them.

She turned and ran back toward the cave, into tunnel and toward the sounds of rocks caving in ahead of her.

"Tyson!" she shouted. "Tyson, can you hear me?"

Then she felt the searing heat of hot air rush toward her skin like an oven. Thick smoke billowed toward her. She pulled her shirt over her mouth to help her breathe.

Then she heard a majestic woof and felt the warmth of Echo brush past her in the tunnel.

"Skylar!" Tyson's voice came to her through the smoke above the sound of the roaring rocks.

"I'm here!" she called.

In an instant she'd reached him and realized he was dragging Daniel's unconscious body along with him.

"I need you to get under his shoulders on one side," he said. "I'll get the other, and we'll carry him out together."

She positioned herself to Daniel's right, Tyson shifted some of Daniel's weight onto her shoulders and together they ran back toward the sunlight.

"What happened?" she shouted.

"When he realized I had him beat, he tried to shoot the explosives and detonate them himself. The explosion blew him back into a wall, knocked him out and started a cave-in. He's barely conscious but alive. There's no way I'm going to let him avoid facing justice."

For a moment the tunnel seemed endless, and she began to fear she'd never escape the thick smoke and tumbling rocks. Then, suddenly, they were running out into the daylight. They carried Daniel down the hill as paramedics ran up to meet them.

"This man took a blow to the back of his head," Tyson told the police and paramedics as they took Daniel from them. "He might also have chemical burns that haven't developed yet. He's the kingpin of a huge drug operation. He's under arrest for murder, kidnapping and drug crimes, and needs to be kept under constant supervision."

Tyson had barely a moment to pause for breath and watch the paramedics carry Daniel down the hill, when Echo came charging up and barreled into them, licking Skylar and Tyson in turn. He knelt down and hugged his K-9 partner.

Tyson turned toward her. He opened his arms. Skylar ran into them. He hugged her hard, lifting her up off her feet before setting her back down on the ground. Tyson kissed her and she kissed him back, without hesitation or fear, and for a long moment they just stood there with their arms wrapped around each other. Then they pulled apart just enough to gaze in each other's faces.

She watched as deeper happiness than she'd ever known pooled in his eyes and met its echo in the beating of her own heart.

Then suddenly she stepped back out of his embrace.

"Your meeting with SAC Bridges!" she cried. "I forgot all about it. What happened?"

"I missed it," Tyson said softly. "When I called your phone and Daniel answered, telling me he'd kidnapped you, I knew that no matter how deeply I cared about my work, that saving your life had to come first." He ran his hand over the back of his neck. "I can only hope that finally capturing the drug kingpin and mastermind of the sabotage and Jason Roque's killer means that Bridges won't shut down the unit."

"I hope not," she said. She stepped forward and wrapped her arms around him.

"But the fact that I missed the meeting probably doesn't bode well for the unit's future," he said. "Especially considering his main concern was that I'm overstretched. It could be the last straw, the perp caught or not." He shook his head. "I'm sorry if the unit is shutting down," Tyson said. "But no matter what happens next I will never regret coming to save you. I want the Rocky Mountain K-9 Unit to succeed and to be its leader. Very, very much. But what I need is you by my side forever. I love you, Skylar. You make me a better man than I ever dreamed I could be."

"I love you too," she said. "I'm sorry I pushed you away. I was afraid of feeling this way about someone. Now, I know I'm more afraid of being without you."

He took her in his arms, she stepped toward him and they hugged tightly.

Then they walked down the hill, hand in hand, with Echo by his side, to face the likely end of the Rocky Mountain K-9 Unit.

# FIFTEEN

The sun was setting as Gavin drove Tyson and Skylar back to the RMKU. Her vehicle had disappeared from where she'd left it, no doubt stolen—and probably by Bernie, though she told Tyson and Gavin that she was grateful if that meant he'd gotten to safety. It was a tight fit with three humans and two dogs in the SUV. Tyson's body ached for a hot meal and a moment of peace to sit on the couch beside Skylar holding her hand. But he needed to go back to the RMKU. He had to find out what had happened with SAC Bridges and then call the man to ask if they could talk.

His unit needed him. Rest would have to wait. Headquarters was dark and empty. That was unusual. A few officers should still be around. Not a single light was on. He turned to tell Gavin to turn on a switch, but Gavin,

Koda and Skylar were nowhere to be found. Had they stopped in the lobby?

Tyson strode to his office and switched on the light.

"Surprise!" a chorus of voices shouted.

He gasped a breath and looked around. The entire K-9 unit, support staff and dogs crowded around his office. Chris held a tablet computer in front of him showing Lucas's beaming face joining them on video call. Skylar, Gavin and Koda appeared in the doorway behind him, and he realized they must've held back, so he'd walk in alone. Had Gavin been tipped off and then signaled Skylar to hold back? Before he could say a word, Jodie pressed a cup of sparkling cider into their hands.

"What is this?" Tyson said. "What are we celebrating?"

"Well, for starters, SAC Bridges loved your proposals for strengthening the RMKU," Nelson said.

"I mean, when he saw you weren't here, he wasn't happy and wanted to leave," Ben said.

"But, I explained to him that Skylar was in danger and you had gone to save her and would very likely be catching the perp responsible for the sabotage to the unit," Jodie said. "That got his interest."

"Then we sat him down," Chris continued the story, "divided your notes between us and went through them point by point."

"He was especially interested in getting the perspective of somebody who was off in the field," Lucas said. "I think he had a lot of misconceptions about that."

"And it helped that you left such detailed notes," Nelson added. "Like you were really thorough. I think he was a little overwhelmed because he kept saying stuff like 'I didn't think of it that way.' And then when he started raising questions we were like 'You're right. We're no ordinary team. But that's what makes us able to do the work we do and we couldn't do it without Tyson.'"

"Then I called into the RMKU when backup arrived," Gavin said, "and they patched me in. I told Bridges you'd made good on your vow to catch the perp sabotaging the unit. After liking your proposals, questioning the team and hearing that, he had all he needed to make a decision. The unit is not being shut down."

Tyson felt as if his breath had been knocked out of his lungs. He leaned back against his desk, feeling Skylar take his hand on one side and Echo press against his leg on the other as if sharing their strength with him. "And that worked?"

"It sure did," Jodie said. "He told us to tell you that he'll be popping into the office on Monday to go over your proposals and chart the course ahead. But to let you know that he's feeling confident in the future of the Rocky Mountain K-9 Unit."

Nelson held his coffee mug aloft.

"To the Rocky Mountain K-9 Unit," Nelson said, "and our fearless leader, Tyson Wilkes!"

"Hear! Hear!" Gavin shouted and they raised their cups aloft.

"And to Dominic Young," Tyson said. He looked over and met Skylar's eyes. "He wasn't perfect. But to those of us who served with him, he was one of us and he was loved." Tyson kept his cup in the air. "And to little Chloe Baker," he added. "We will find you. We will rescue you and catch your mother's murderer and Kate's attacker and bring that person to justice. We won't rest until we do."

"So say all of us," Ben agreed and they held their cups aloft.

Two weeks later, Tyson stood in the parking lot of the Rocky Mountain K-9 Unit, beside his shiny new SUV, and waited for

Skylar to arrive. Beyond him the mountains were awash in a gorgeous vista of orange and gold. In his hand he held a bouquet of long-stemmed roses. At his feet sat Echo, patient and looking very dapper with a sparkling black bow tie.

Tyson's heart was racing inside his chest like a kid on Christmas Eve.

He glanced to the dusky sky above as prayers of thanksgiving bubbled up inside him.

So much had happened since the day he and Skylar had confessed they loved each other at Fault Cave. Daniel Young had survived his injuries and was now in prison awaiting trial. Thanks to Skylar's stellar police work, law enforcement had amassed a mountain of evidence not only showing how Daniel had been the kingpin behind the drug smuggling operation, but how he'd also orchestrated an escalating series of attacks on Tyson and the RMKU in revenge for the death of his brother, Dominic. And law enforcement agencies across the region were now in the process of dismantling his entire operation. Bernie for his part had walked into a random Denver police station to return Skylar's car and confess to stealing it to escape the situation he'd been forced into by Daniel. He was now in a rehab program, on probation and planning to marry his girlfriend, who had started coming to Skylar's support group.

Shiloh was thriving in his training under Jodie's tutelage and Chase had been placed with a new RMKU member who'd transferred in from the FBI's K-9 program.

Kate Montgomery would soon be moving out of the rehab center and with Skylar's help found a rental for herself and Cocoa in Montana. She was planning on bringing a few drawing pads with her, hoping that sketching the scenery around her would be healing, not only in helping her to fully regain her memory but that maybe she'd draw something that would trigger what had been buried inside her since that tragic April night when baby Chloe had been kidnapped.

And true to his word, after grilling Tyson about his plans, SAC Bridges had authorized making the RMKU a permanent fixture in the Rocky Mountain law enforcement community.

But despite all the busyness, Tyson and Skylar kept creating time for each other, every day. They went for long walks on the weekend, cooked dinner together whenever they could, met at each other's offices for lunches and ended each night in a long conversation on the phone together. They'd even lent each other their favorite books to read.

*Lord, You've blessed me far more than I've ever imagined possible.*

There was just one more thing his life needed to be complete.

His heart rate quickened as he saw Skylar pull into the parking lot. While he knew headquarters and the training center were still full of colleagues training the new dogs, and working on new cases and implementing some of the new protocols, right now the parking lot was so empty it was as if they were the only ones there.

The driver's-side door opened, Skylar stepped out and he felt his mouth go dry. She was dressed simply, in a green leather jacket with her long red hair falling in loose waves around her shoulders. She turned to him and a curious smile curled on her lips as she spotted first the flowers and then Echo's bow tie. And Tyson knew that nothing he'd ever seen, not even the majesty of the sunset over the Rocky Mountains in their splendor, could ever compare to the beauty of her smile.

*Okay, here goes nothing.* He swallowed hard and walked over.

She met him in the middle of the lot. They stopped there, toe to toe.

"Hey," she said and smiled.

"Hi," he said, and for a moment it was all he could manage.

She slipped her arms around him in a hug, he hugged her back and their lips met in a kiss. Then they pulled apart and she looked down at Echo. Echo's tail thumped in greeting.

"Well, someone's looking very fancy today," she said. "Is it a special occasion?"

"I have very good news for you," Tyson said, "and an important question."

"Okay," she said.

The curiosity that quirked her smile spread to her eyes.

"SAC Bridges is going to send you an email later today," Tyson said. "We're re-opening the RMKU to new recruits. We've gone over your application and unanimously decided that we'd like you to join the unit. You're an incredible cop. You're dedicated and determined. Everyone is just thrilled at the prospect of having you join the team."

Her hand rose to her lips. Her eyes shone. "Really?"

"Yeah," he said. "SAC Bridges is going to be the one to approach you with the formal offer and details, because you and I have a personal relationship. But he gave me permission to tell you now. Also, I won't be your training officer. We're going to promote Nelson to take on more of the training and supervisory work. It was one of the proposals to get others on the team to share more in the responsibility of running the RMKU. We'll delay your start for six months in order for him to get up to speed and you'll report to him directly."

He watched as she closed her eyes and prayed a silent prayer of thanksgiving to God. Then, when she opened her eyes, he took her left hand in his and squeezed it tightly.

"Thank you," she said. "Thank you so much. I'm so excited to join the team."

"The team is excited to have you," he said. "We truly believe you'll make us all better."

She glanced down at the roses in his other hand. "So that's what these are for?" she asked.

"Not quite," he said. Then he blew out a long breath, once again, the words he wanted to say seeming so hard to find. "SAC Bridges asked me about the status of our relationship. It's not a problem at all for him—he just wanted everything to be clear up front. He asked me where I saw our relationship headed. And I knew the answer, immediately. But I said I couldn't tell him until I'd talked it over with you."

In Tyson's life he'd made a lot of brave decisions. He'd leaped from an airplane over a war zone. He'd walked into a room full of mercenaries to obtain the release of a hostage. He'd run into battle to save his colleagues. And yet, nothing he'd ever done felt more important or had higher stakes than the action he was about to take now.

Tyson knelt down on one knee.

"I love you, Skylar," he said. "You make me happier than I've ever been and a better man than I ever imagined I could be. I want to support you in your plans and cheer you on as you reach your goals. I want to come home to you every night, celebrate with you when we're happy and hold you when we're sad. I want to spend the rest of my life by your side. I know it's only been a few days, and so if you're not ready to make that decision yet I understand. But I want to marry you and I've never been more certain of anything else in my life."

Tears slipped from the corners of her beautiful eyes. She squeezed his hand, then he stood and she wrapped her arms around him.

"I'm in love with you too, Tyson," she said. "You're the most amazing man I've ever met. And yes, I'll marry you."

"Really?" he asked.

She chuckled. "Definitely."

He kissed her lips and held her tight. Then they walked into the RMKU with Echo by his side to tell the team the good news.

\* \* \* \* \*

Dear Reader,

I've always loved calendars. I have an old steamer trunk in my office where I keep copies of my books and years' worth of calendars. Ever since I was little I've looked forward to each new calendar and the moment it arrived I always turned straight to April to see what the picture would be for my birthday.

I used to take pictures of friends, family and the world around me and turn them into an annual calendar. One year I took a long road trip from Toronto to Florida and back, making dozens of stops along the way, including in Washington, D.C., Chicago, Philadelphia, a US Army base in North Carolina, and Atlanta, taking pictures along the way.

I was surprised when I opened my mailbox this week and found a calendar in it from a nearby community church.

I turned to the month this book is coming out and the verse jumped out at me: "Come unto me, all ye that labor and are heavy laden, and I will give you rest." (Matthew 11:28) It seemed to fit so well for how Tyson is feeling at the start of this book.

I hope you find the rest you need from the things that are wearing you down, and the right people to help you through. Thank you again for your letters, emails and messages. They always encourage me and fill me with joy. Thank you, as always, for sharing this journey with me.

*Maggie*

# HARLEQUIN
## PLUS

Announcing a **BRAND-NEW** multimedia subscription service for romance fans like you!

---

## **Read, Watch and Play.**

Experience the easiest way to get the romance content you crave.

Start your **FREE 7 DAY TRIAL** at
<u>www.harlequinplus.com/freetrial</u>.